MIDNIGHT MIS

Tessa Bellamy kne⸻⸻⸻⸻⸻⸻e alone with Lord Hartfield so late at night in his room, much less be having this scandalous conversation with him.

But he smiled ironically and took her hand in his and mockingly asked, "Will you do me the dubious honor of becoming my wife, Miss Bellamy? I promise to shower upon you every comfort your money can buy, and if you give me your pledge to do nothing to disgrace me, I shall give you mine not to dose you with deadly laudanum."

Tessa's heart was beating so hard and fast in her breast that she knew he must feel it in her pulse.

"What would you do if I said yes?" she queried recklessly.

And almost instantly she had her answer as she heard his mirthless laugh and felt his arms around her. . . .

THE FORTUNE HUNTER

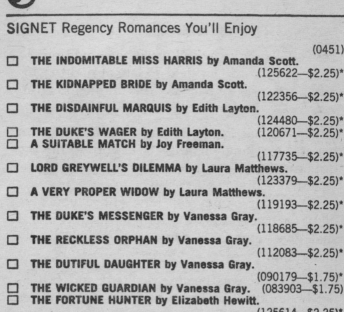

THE
FORTUNE
HUNTER

by
Elizabeth Hewitt

A SIGNET BOOK
NEW AMERICAN LIBRARY
TIMES MIRROR

SIGNET TRADEMARK REG. U.S. PAT. OFF. AND FOREIGN COUNTRIES
REGISTERED TRADEMARK—MARCA REGISTRADA
HECHO EN CHICAGO, U.S.A.

SIGNET, SIGNET CLASSIC, MENTOR, PLUME, MERIDIAN and NAL BOOKS
are published by The New American Library, Inc.,
1633 Broadway, New York, New York 10019

First Printing, November, 1983

1 2 3 4 5 6 7 8 9

PRINTED IN THE UNITED STATES OF AMERICA

Chapter One

"Midnight has come and gone, coz, and not a single disaster has occurred, unless you count the two waiters from the agency that arrived castaway and had to be replaced at the last minute," said the Honorable Reverend Colin McAffe with a grin that women described as adorable, and which a few of his superiors in the Church regarded as ill-suited to a man of the cloth. "The wager, I think, is mine," he added with a beguiling smile.

Like all the McAffes, Colin was possessed of exceptionally good looks and had learned from the cradle how to use them to advantage, but his cousin Tessa was proof against his charm. Though surnamed Bellamy, Tessa was a McAffe through her mother and could appreciate the allure of her cousin without falling victim to it.

"I am certain that the archbishop would say that it is vulgar for a clergyman to wager," she admonished him, "so I shan't bother about the payment of it."

They stood together sipping champagne punch in a mercifully empty refreshment room adjacent to the magnificent ballroom in the Bellamys' elegant London mansion. Both were content to listen to the music rather than to take part in the revels being held in honor of the betrothal of Tessa's younger sister Letitia to Viscount Torrance, heir to an earldom, a modest fortune, and estates in Shropshire.

Even a less-than-astute observer would have noticed at once the family resemblance between Colin and Tessa, and an unkind observer might have remarked that nature had been more generous to the male than the female. Both had well-sculptured features with prominent cheekbones and large, clear expressive eyes, but seen side by side with her cousin, Tessa appeared to be only a pale copy of the glorious original. Where his eyes were an arresting blue, hers were simply dark gray; where his hair was as black as a moonless night, hers could only be termed brown. His complexion was interestingly pallid; hers wanted color.

The sad truth was that Tessa had taken more from her father's family than her mother's, and the Bellamys were far more noted for their quick, intuitive minds, superior understanding, and ability to get on in the world than for anything remarkable in their faces or forms. Nonetheless, it was these traits which had, in only three generations, brought them from simple yeoman stock to intermarriage with the cream of the aristocracy, and Tessa was glad enough with what she had. She respected a quick mind over a pretty face and had, in compensation for any deficiencies in the latter, developed the abilities she felt were her own best features. She was in any case considered by most a very handsome young woman and only suffered in comparison to her mother, her cousins, or her younger sister, who had inherited the McAffe beauty in full measure.

"And I am certain that Mamma would say that it was vulgar for you to wager at all," Letitia Bellamy said now as she came into the room. She sat down in a chair near her cousin and sister and began to fan herself vigorously. "La, who would have thought it would be so hot in October?"

"Tired of being the principal attraction of the evening already?" Colin quizzed gently. "And here I had suspected you of waiting until now to accept Torrance so that your betrothal would be the talk of the Little Season."

"That's a monstrously cruel thing to say, Colin," she said with a consciously adorable pout. "If I am fortunate enough to have the means to marry where I please and thought it best to be certain of my feelings before committing myself to anything so crucial to my future, I think I should be commended, not condemned."

"Which," said Tessa with a smile for Colin, "means that she needed to be certain that a viscount who was heir to an earldom was the best she would do."

Letitia tossed her raven curls and glared at her sister with eyes that were as richly blue as Colin's. "I think you are both horrid," she said, but she was used to such treatment from her cousin and sister, and she did not really mind their cynicism, especially as there were, in the words of both, elements of truth. Letitia, after all, was a Bellamy too.

Possessed of a dowry that had caused gasps of pleasure to issue from the lips of most fortune hunters, and co-heiress with her sister of a far greater amount, Letitia had embarked on her first season secure that she would be declared an "Incomparable" and much sought after, and had determined to be wed to her greatest advantage by the next season. It was not that she was not fond of Lord Torrance: his doting, complaisant manner exactly suited her more dominant personality. But the truth was that if he had not been favorably connected with most of the important aristocracy in the kingdom, his suit might well not have prospered.

"I think it is you who are horrid, Letty," countered her sister. "Or at any rate, foolish. I would have expected you to have better social sense than to invite Sir Richard Cassidy when you knew that Constance Hartfield would be attending. Mamma and I worked very hard to make this ball a success, and you risk its ruin by inviting an unfortunate scene."

Letitia was not concerned. "Oh, pooh," she said in her best grand manner, "it is not so much that I invited Sir Richard and Connie that you mind, it is that Connie came tonight with her husband. Who could have guessed that Hartfield would pick today to return to town? No one has set eyes on him forever."

"I am sure you only sent Sir Richard a card because Constance asked you to do so," Tessa persisted. "He is hardly a friend of our family. Knowing he would be here, *she* should have known better than to bring Hartfield in tow, for your sake if not for her own."

"One might have supposed that she would find it a trifle awkward to be in the same room with her husband and the man with whom she has been setting everyone's tongue wagging," Colin concurred. "But in fairness to Letitia," he added, "If every hostess worried about wives and husbands running into their lovers on dance floors, the company on most nights would be depressingly thin."

"I don't care what concerns other hostesses," Tessa said, casting a quelling glance at her cousin. "Lady Hartfield's behavior oversteps the bounds even of a morality which advocates arranged marriages and closes its eyes to discreet adultery."

"You are more preachy than Colin," Letitia told her in a voice that affected boredom. "If he takes your lead, perhaps he will be the Archbishop one day instead of a mere secretary."

This speech was mildly insulting to Colin, but he was not at all offended. A young man with few self-delusions, he had taken orders two years ago not so much from a deep-felt vocation as because he was the youngest of the Earl of Dexter's four sons and had had the need of a respectable and acceptable occupation.

Though Colin's religious beliefs were sound and deeply held, he would have been wretched performing pastoral duties in a country living; he loved good books, good music, good food, and good friends. London was his natural territory and the ballrooms of the ton were his principal habitat. Thus when his eldest brother, the current earl, had procured for him the post of secretary (one of several) to the Archbishop of Canterbury, he had jumped at the opportunity, though his income was little more than that of the meanest living at his brother's disposal.

"And if I do," he said to Letitia, "you will have to learn a bit of decorum, Letty. It won't do for an archbishop to have a rackety first cousin."

Letitia made a face at him and he gave her a lazy smile in turn. Letitia might be a treat for any man's eyes, but he frankly did not envy Lord Torrance, for she was as headstrong as she was lovely and ambitious. He was one of the few members of the family who openly declared her spoiled and self-centered, not even a little deceived by her pretty smile or languishing glances.

If this were so, it was not so very surprising. Letitia was seldom crossed. What she could not achieve through the unblushing use of her beauty, she obtained through the strength of her will. She and Tessa were not precisely at odds, but the elder sister had little influence over the younger, and even well-meant advice from that quarter was seldom heeded.

Sir Edwin Bellamy, more at home in the exclusively male precincts of Gray's Inn, where, as one of the nation's leading barristers, he had chambers, left the matter of the morals and manners of his daughters to the jurisdiction of his wife, Lady Frances. Lady Frances, who above all things detested fuss and was in any case a bit partial to her younger daughter, usually gave in to Letitia's wishes at the first glistening of a tear in her lovely eyes, or the beginnings of a frown.

Tessa had objected strongly to Letitia's friendship with Constance Hartfield, feeling the dashing young marchioness was just a might *too* dashing for an eighteen-year-old girl in her first season. In spite of six years of marriage in which Lady Hartfield had lived more often apart from her husband than with him, and in constant succession taken a number of socially prominent men as lovers, she had never placed herself beyond the pale and was received everywhere. This was partly due to her discretion and largely due to the fact that she was the only child of the Duke of Gillane, one of the richest and most powerful men in England. But of late Constance's behavior was not so easily winked at even by the most morally liberal; she made little secret of her passion for Sir Richard, and defied the ton to condemn her.

This had not happened yet, and according to Lady Frances Bellamy, would not. "You may depend upon it," she had said to her elder daughter when Tessa had broached the subject, "Lady Hartfield will stop short of utterly ruining herself, and the world will give her just that little extra leeway for the sake of her father." Tessa had felt that this was a poor reason for allowing Constance's influence in Letitia's life, but Lady Frances, aware that Letitia would put up a great fuss if separated from Lady Hartfield, waved aside her concerns, saying that Letitia was sensible and not impressionable and would in any case soon be in the care of her new husband and not likely to find trouble.

This vexed Tessa, but as she could not prevent it, she did what she could to counter the marchioness's influence, though she doubted that much she said was heeded. If asked, she would have said that she loved her sister, but there were too many differences in personality, character, and general outlook for closeness. Nonetheless, if Tessa did not understand Letitia, she was concerned for her, fearing that if she continued to have her head too much, she would become just such a one as Lady Hartfield: beautiful, spoiled, hedonistic, and forever skirting social disaster.

"Even if Lord Hartfield had not come here tonight," Tessa insisted, "Constance is the volatile sort who will kick up a dust if it suits her, without a thought for the friends she might be embarrassing."

Colin drained off the last of his punch and sat back in his chair, crossing one shapely leg over the other. "I wonder, Letitia, that you let yourself be used as a source of rendezvous by Costance Hartfield," he said in his soft drawling voice that commented more than criticized. "If she does fall into ruin, as she has been promising to do anytime this past year, you wouldn't much like it if she took you with her."

"I wish you might hear how self-righteous you both sound," Letitia said peevishly. "You are forever prosing on about how selfish I am and how inconsiderate of the feelings of others, yet you condemn poor Connie on the strength of mere gossip."

"*Poor* Connie!" Tessa said scathingly. "That is the last adjective *I* should have used to describe Constance Hartfield."

"And that quite proves my point," Letitia said triumphantly. "Because she is rich and beautiful and highborn, it is assumed that she cannot need the sympathy or pity of anyone. Yet she has confided to me that she is the unhappiest of creatures! Tied in marriage to a man who would rather spend his time among pigs and sheep like a paid steward than take his place at her side in the ton. He leaves her to fend for herself without a care as to how she gets on in the world. Is it any wonder that her heart is susceptible to the consolation of Another?"

Tessa regarded her lovely sister with a jaundiced eye. A lifetime of histrionics from that quarter had taught her that the only way to prevent a full-scale dramatic scenario was to slap down any hint of melodrama with a dose of reality. "Is that what Constance told you?" she asked disdainfully. "Pity wretched Connie, bored and neglected? Fending for herself in the luxury of forty rooms on Grosvenor Square with a skeleton staff of twenty?"

"Luxuries are not everything," Letitia said loftily. "Gold and silver make cold bedfellows."

Tessa and Colin exchanged glances, and the gravity of each was overset. Letitia pursed her lips censoriously. "You would not laugh if you were trapped in a marriage which was In Name Only."

"Then I shall take care not to be such a fool as to contract marriage with a man who would have it so," Tessa said dampeningly.

Letitia shook her head, too caught up in the romance of her friend's story to give it up easily, in spite of the ridicule of her unfeeling family. "Constance believed she was contracting a love match, but was sadly deceived."

"Stuff and nonsense, Letty," said Colin. "Everyone knows that Hartfield was pockets to let when he married Constance. His father left matters in such a state when he cut his stick that the family was put out of Caster Priory and nearly chucked into the street."

"Constance believed in his love," Letitia insisted stubbornly. "Neither of you like Connie and are unfairly prejudiced against her. I suppose it is because Papa was a friend of Lord Hartfield's papa, and if you ask me, he must have been a shocking loose screw to have gamed away a fortune and left his wife and children destitute, so I do not think it is surprising that his son is just such a one."

Colin knit his brow. "I never heard that this Hartfield was a gamester."

"He is not," Letitia conceded, "but he is cold and has no proper feeling."

"You are no better acquainted with him than I am," Tessa said ascerbically, "and I've had a half-dozen polite conversations and listened to gossip from people who are not likely to be objective about his character. Constance can claim the distinction that I have come to dislike her quite on her own merit."

"Hartfield was only a year or so before me at Oxford, but I can't say I know him very well, either," Colin put in. "He's always been rather a close sort. Still, it was common knowledge that his father was a rip who'd take a wager on the number of raindrops to come out of a spout. Don't much care for the dowager, either. Always playing off airs and graces," he added with a purposeful look at his younger cousin. "Makes her wearing to know, but I must say I rather like the sister, Lady Margaret."

"Meg Caster is a dead bore," Letitia said in a tone of dismissal.

"That sounds like another of Constance's pronouncements," said Tessa. "Meg is a bit shy and doesn't bring herself to notice much, but she is very nice."

Letitia gave a stagy shudder. "I would rather be called 'horrid' than 'nice.' What a bland word and how exactly it describes Lady Margaret."

Colin grinned and patted Letitia's hand. "You may rest easy, love. You *are* far more likely to be described as horrid than nice."

Letitia made a face at him and stood up. "It doesn't matter what you or Tess think of Connie, for I don't believe she thinks much of you, either. *Everyone* knows that Hartfield is a cold fish and it is just one more burden that Constance must bear that some will take his part against all reason."

"Well," said Colin, who was facing the door, "here comes 'poor' Connie now, and though I can't say she looks particularly burdened to me, no doubt you know best and will be glad of the chance to give her a bit of comfort."

A statuesque brunette with features to equal any the McAffe blood could produce came toward them, wearing a startling shade of violet which only some-one with her complexion and coloring would have dared wear. The silk clung suggestively to her frame with every sinewy movement.

Letitia watched her approach with an expectant smile and Colin with avid appreciation, but Tessa was only wryly amused that a woman who had nearly made herself notorious would wish to make tongues wag all the more by dampening her petticoats, espe-cially when the naturally voluptuous curves of her body made this patently unnecessary.

But it was not Colin's admiration or Letitia's appro-bation that Constance sought when she came into the room. Her gaze went at once to Tessa, and a knowing smile tilted the corners of her full lips. If Constance did not like Tessa any more than that young woman did her, she did respect her.

Both women were realists who knew what they wished from life, and neither was afraid to take a step that would achieve it. The thing that set them irrevocably apart was that Tessa's needs and desires were tempered by her principles, and no such barri-ers existed for the beautiful daughter of the Duke of Gillane, an only child, spoiled and pandered to from the cradle by doting older parents; no ties of love or blood, no bond of friendship ever stood in the way of the things that mattered to Constance.

Lady Hartfield gave Tessa and then Colin a brief nod and then turned her attention to the uncritical Letitia. "I have tracked you down at last, pet," she said with her charming smile. "You have been so surrounded tonight by everyone wishing you happy that it has been all but impossible for your friends to exchange more than a word with you." She linked her arm in Letitia's. "But I am more determined than the others and now that I have found you I intend to take you off for a comfortable coze in one of those delightful little anterooms near the musicians." She cast a brief challenging glance at Tessa through her thick lashes. "Tess is giving me her black looks, Letty, but we shan't be deterred by her notions of propriety."

"Letty may please herself," Tessa said languidly. "She knows well enough what is due her guests without me to tell her."

"If it is my ball," Letitia said, rising to the bait, "then I think I may be allowed to enjoy myself, but," she added apologetically for Constance, "I am promised this set to Torrance, and," she said, nodding toward the revelers who had drifted into the room at the end of the last dance and were now moving back toward the ballroom, "I think it about to be formed."

"I won't hear of that as an excuse," Constance said. "Torrance shall have you for the rest of his life. For the next half-hour it is I who lay claim to your notice."

"If it is a question of having no one to dance with," Colin said sweetly, "I should be honored to stand up with you, Lady Hartfield. Though levity is in general frowned upon in my profession, an exception for duty's sake is certainly allowed."

Constance gave him a tight smile, undeceived by his wide innocent eyes or the blandness of his tone. "You are most generous, Mr. McAffe—"

"Colin is noted for his generosity," Tessa interjected. "In fact, I fear," she added with a faint nod toward Letitia, "that the whole of my family is beset with an excess of it."

"A failing you may congratulate yourself on not sharing," countered Constance waspishly. She turned her back to the cousins and again addressed Letitia. "Come, dearest, I have several delicious *on-dits* to share with you, and you must tell me every sweet promise that Torrance has made to you tonight."

Mortified by the behavior of her cousin and sister, Letitia no longer hesitated but with a toss of her black curls turned on her heel and left the room with Constance, in the wake of the last of those who were returning to the dance.

"Assuming that poor Torrance has had the opportunity to say anything at all to Letty tonight," Tessa said acidly as soon as they were out of earshot. "Heavens, but I cannot abide that woman. I don't wonder that Hartfield spends all of his time wherever she is not. If I had to live with that witch, I should probably end in poisoning her."

"It is more likely that she would poison you," Colin said. "She's the one without scruples. Aren't you promised to m'brother Stephen for this dance?"

"Am I? Would you be kind, Colin, and find him and ask him to excuse me? This has been a hectic day—in fact, a hectic week—and I think I would like to sit out a bit longer."

"Oh, Stephen won't mind. He'd as soon play backgammon with Colonel Tentrees anytime," Colin said with more honesty than tact. "But I am bespoken to Miss Collins, an ethereal little beauty with two thousand a year, I am told, so you are on your own, my girl. I warn you, though, if you are still here when this set is done, I shall have to speak to you on the evils of sloth."

"You would do better to prepare a sermon for yourself on the dangers of avarice and envy," she called after him as he left the room.

Her weariness was no false excuse. Most of the planning for the ball and all of the necessary last-minute details that had needed attending to had fallen to her shoulders, as had been the case since she had come out of the schoolroom. While her mother and sister spent most of the day in darkened rooms with cucumber compresses on their eyes to prepare them for the revels of the evening, Tessa had dealt with florists and wine merchants, conferred with the butler, and soothed a harassed cook.

Tessa did not at all resent the inactivity of her mother or sister and would herself have found such stillness more than her patience could bear. It didn't matter to her that her complexion was a bit brown from her walk last week in the sun, or that a night spent wakefully going over last-minute details for the ball had left her with fine lines beneath her eyes. In fact she enjoyed the activity and welcomed it, knowing that she was a rather managing sort of female and feeling that this fault might as well be turned to good use.

Not that she really thought it a fault in a woman to be decisive and self-contained: she simply knew that her habit of trying to arrange the lives of those she loved to what she perceived as their advantage was not always appreciated.

She smiled at her own folly, thinking that at least Letitia was about to escape her dominion. That did not concern Tessa overmuch, for they had never been truly close, though only three years separated them in age. What did concern her was Letitia's growing self-confidence, which was becoming almost a vanity and was making her heedless of any counsel but her own. Tessa did not share her mother's assumption that Torrance would direct and advise Letitia, for his very besottedness made him bow to her wishes in all things. Tessa genuinely feared that, unchecked, Letitia might become another Constance, a self-centered hedonist and a hardened care-for-nobody.

Tessa was sitting slumped in her chair staring down at her folded fan in her lap, but a sound made her look up to find the Marquis of Hartfield had entered the room and was regarding her quizzically. Perhaps because it was his wife who had just figured poorly in her thoughts, she was more startled

than the situation called for and stood up so abruptly
that she nearly toppled her chair.

"I beg your pardon, Miss Bellamy," Lord Hartfield
said, coming over to her. "I didn't mean to startle
you so."

"It . . . it isn't your fault," she answered, her
voice a bit clipped with embarrassment. "I'm afraid I
was rather lost in . . ." She recalled her last thought
and flushed slightly and was instantly furious with
herself for this uncharacteristically missish behavior.

"Idle speculation?" he finished for her with a dry
inflection and the faintest upward lift to the corners
of his mouth.

Though she had not been dwelling specifically on
the gossip that always swirled about Lord Hartfield
and his wife, she understood him well enough to be
discomfited. There could be little doubt that his own
name had figured on most of those lips present since
his unexpected arrival tonight.

As if he were reading her thoughts, his smile
broadened and his rather heavy lids dropped even
further, hiding his expression completely.

Tessa reflected that he had no doubt had a great
deal of practice in hiding his feelings, and her very
next thought, following rapidly on this, was that
Constance Hartfield was a fool. The marquis was
certainly not the most handsome man of Tessa's
acquaintance—her cousin Colin, for one, outshone
him—but there was something about his finely carved
features and dignified but not rigid carriage that was
certainly arresting. His dark blond hair was cut se-
verely in a brutus and brushed forward to feather
his well-shaped ears and wide, intelligent brow. His
eyes, which told her so little, were an odd shade of
light gray which she had noted previously could
seem almost metallic in certain lights. His well-made
form showed off his superbly cut evening clothes to
perfection, and there was no padding to his shoul-

ders or a corset to nip in his waist—of that she was certain.

But the simple fact that he was a married man whom she found quite to her taste was no cause for her foolish reaction to him, and she took herself firmly in hand. She straightened her back and made herself meet his gaze squarely. "Actually," she said at last in a matter-of-fact voice, "I was thinking of my feet and how tired they are from rushing about all day and dancing all night."

At that, he put back his head slightly and laughed, the shuttered lids rising to take her in more fully. She thought his features completely transformed to something very near male beauty, and realized with some surprise that though they had been vaguely acquainted for most of her life, this was the first time she could recall hearing his laughter.

When he spoke, even his voice seemed to have a lighter quality. "How delightfully prosaic! Then I shall admit to you that I have been thinking much the same thing for the last half-hour or so. I was at Redfield, an estate of mine in Yorkshire, at this time three nights ago and have been traveling almost ever since. I want nothing so much as a quiet room, a comfortable chair, and a stool to put up my feet."

He paused and his eyes beheld her with curiosity and, quite decidedly, admiration. "One does not, however, usually discuss such matters with lovely young women at stylish balls. After all the fencing and false flattery that usually passes for conversation, I should think your friends must find you a refreshing delight."

" 'Refreshing' is not the adjective that is generally applied to my plain speaking," she replied coolly, not certain whether he was flirting with her or quizzing her. But the smile that he gave her at these words was quite infectious and she could not help returning it, adding, "My sister Letty is convinced that it is mere affectation to bring notice to myself, but the truth is that I can't see the point in saying one thing when I mean another, unless it would be hurtful to another to do so."

"And you do not consider that refreshing?" he asked, incredulous. "I fear I have been out of the world too long, if society has taken up honesty in favor of subterfuge and dissembling."

Tessa laughed. "You would be sadly out of step if you judged society by my example," she admitted ruefully, and without thought, added, "But if I were poor Miss Bellamy instead of rich Miss Bellamy, I should be deemed odd instead of original, and shunned rather than courted. There is a degree of latitude given to heiresses that is not permitted to lesser mortals." The words were spoken with dry self-mockery and she had no notion of the meaning they might hold for him until she saw the smile fade from his eyes.

She had certainly not meant to hint at his own wife's behavior and the manner in which the world chose to ignore if not precisely condone it. She felt an urge to stammer an apology, but knew that would be awkward and perhaps make her blunder even worse. It should not matter to her what he now thought of her, but she had just contradicted her own maxim that honesty should not be carried to the point of being unnecessarily hurtful, and she must look a fool as well as deliberately acid-tongued. She strongly regretted her unfortunate words and would have regained his good opinion if she had known how to do so.

"The world is seldom fair to those who cannot buy its kindness," he said, but so levelly that Tessa could not be certain if he mocked her, himself, or was just generally cynical. "Have you seen Lady Hartfield?" he asked abruptly. "I came here hoping to find her. I *am* tired and it is time we left."

"She is gone with Letty to one of the anterooms," Tessa replied promptly, glad of any change of subject.

"They are become particular friends since Letty's come out, and they wished for privacy to talk. I am sure you will still find her there. The rooms are in the hall just by the musicians' gallery."

He nodded and thanked her with the politeness of a stranger, but something seemed to hold him. He turned to leave and then turned back again. "Was this last season your sister's first?" he asked finally; surprising Tessa with the incongruity of his question.

"Yes. Why?"

"I thought she seemed rather young," he replied, which gave her no notion of what was in his mind.

"Are you perhaps thinking that she is a bit immature to be a companion to your wife?" she prompted archly.

His sudden transforming smile flashed again, but this time with a trace of irony. "Actually, I was thinking that Constance is too mature for her," he said with some of Tessa's own plain speaking, "which is not at all the same thing. You may think it odd in me to say this, Miss Bellamy, but I should not encourage that closeness." He accorded her the briefest of bows and left the room.

Tessa thoughtfully watched him leave, not sure just what her opinion was of the Marquis of Hartfield. Though their fathers had been friends, closeness between the families had not existed until a mere five years ago, when the marquis had purchased the house next to their own for his mother and sister to live in after the sale of Caster Priory and the family's former home in Grosvenor Square. Tessa had, of course, met him before that, but most of their meetings had been brief and public, so that in a way she felt she knew him more by repute than acquaintance.

She did not care to base her judgment on the previous judgments of others, but it was naturally impossible not to do so to some extent. The difficulty in the case of Lord Hartfield was that the report of his character differed so greatly among those who were close to him. Her own father termed him a man of character, decisive, responsible, and trustworthy; Hartfield's sister Margaret called him goodhearted, generous, and considerate. But the two women who must surely be the most important in the marquis' life, his mother and his wife, gave him a very different sort of character. The dowager marchioness was at times heard to declare her elder offspring unfeeling and thoughtless of a poor widowed mother's feelings; his wife—well, when Constance spoke of her husband as cold, mean-spirited, and a care-for-nobody, she was being more charitable toward him than was usual for her. All that Tessa's own experience had taught her to date was that he did not easily give away his thoughts and that his mind was quick and his manner occasionally arrogant.

On the whole, though, Tessa was inclined to look upon him favorably. In the first place, he *was* a very attractive man, and in the second, if she was going to accept the opinions of others, she would certainly take those of her father and Margaret Caster over those of the dowager and Constance Hartfield.

Both the dowager and Constance were to Tessa prime examples of the pitfalls that great beauty held for a woman. The dowager, in whose now lined features could still be traced the form of her once great beauty, had responded to the pampering and adulation that her loveliness had brought her by becoming not so much vain as self-centered. She saw nothing and no one around her except as they affected herself, praising all that contributed to her comfort and conformed to her will, and damning all that did not. She was emotionally manipulative and given to a self-dramatization that Tessa had already noted becoming visible in her own sister's character.

Constance, on the other hand, was just plain selfish. Or at least that was Tessa's opinion of a woman who ruthlessly trampled the feelings and pride of others to get what she wished. To give her some due, though, Tessa didn't believe that Constance was even aware most of the time of the devastation that she left in her wake. If she had her way, everything was delightful to her and no black cloud was permitted to dampen her spirits.

It was for this reason as much as Lady Hartfield's sad want of moral standards that Tessa deplored her friendship with Letitia. For all the airs and graces that Letitia had taken on since her come-out, and the little vanities that were arising from the admiration she received, Letitia was yet an innocent in the ways of the world and a stranger to the disillusionment that so often came from living within it. Tessa knew she could not protect her sister forever, and for that matter, Letitia certainly possessed the ability to fend for herself, but Tessa would have preferred that Letitia's lessons in life not be delivered with the brutality of which she knew women like Constance Hartfield were capable.

In fact, it was wise for any person of delicate sensibility or moral righteousness to avoid the company of either of the Hartfields. Between them, the Marquis and Marchioness of Hartfield had provided society with most of its whispered Crim. Con. stories and *on-dits* since the onset of their marriage nearly six years ago.

In birth and breeding, Jonathan Hartfield was a superb match for the daughter of the Duke of Gillane, but in fortune their match could only be termed a *mésalliance*. It was well known that at the time of their marriage the Caster family was so destitute that the shadow of the Fleet actually loomed above them. It was not very surprising that the world regarded Hartfield as a successful fortune hunter and credited to at least a degree Constance's claim that he was responsible for the dissolution of their marriage.

But Tessa, because her father had assisted the young marquis to put his affairs in order as best he could on the death of his father, knew a bit more of

their story than did the average person and knew
that if there was blame in the matter, it was equally
if not entirely Constance's.

The duke had rigorously opposed the match, not
so much because of Hartfield's want of fortune as for
fear of the gamester's taint. The Duke of Gillane was
principally noted for two things, however. He was
one of the richest and most powerful of the country's
handful of dukes and he doted on his only child to
the point that it won him criticism rather than
approbation.

And Constance had wanted the match every bit as
much as had Jonathan. Tessa was not certain how
the couple had carried the day, for it was not a
subject her father chose to discuss even with his
own beloved and curious daughter, but she rather
thought that there was something about an elopement and even the hushed hint of a seduction. In
any event, they had been wed with full pomp and
the ducal blessing.

But if the felicity in their marriage had lasted beyond
the wedding journey, there had been no outward
evidence of this. From the very beginning of the
resumption of their lives in the ton, it had been clear
that the pair were bonded to each other by little
more than a common name and a shared address.
Even this was reduced when two years ago Lord
Hartfield had abandoned town pursuits to live principally on the various estates of the duke.

There was very little wonder then that the unexpected arrival of the marquis among them, amazingly,
on the arm of his lovely wayward wife, had caused a
sensation that would keep the entire ton abuzz for a
sennight at the least. Nor was it remarkable that
Tessa had feared the occurrence of some unnamed
social disaster, for all the elements of high melodrama were certainly present. But all had gone quite
smoothly and her vague fears were now at last
allayed.

Again the music from the ballroom died away and first one wilting couple and then another came into the room to escape the heat of the filled ballroom and to find refreshment. Tessa acknowledged their greetings but did not bestir herself to join them. She knew it was time that she ceased indulging herself and returned to her duties toward their guests, and reluctantly she rose to return to the ballroom. As she reached the door, she met Letitia coming in on the arm of Lord Torrance. Both were flushed from the dance and the unexpected warmth of the night, but Tessa paid no heed to this until the thought came to her that Letitia had intended to sit out this dance to have her *tête-à-tête* with Constance.

Tessa started to enter the ballroom, but some instinct—or perhaps it was intuition—made her return to the refreshment room. Letitia was again showing off her huge emerald engagement ring to the admiring sighs of her friends, but Tessa managed to engage her attention long enough to ask if she had misunderstood her intention when she had left earlier with Constance Hartfield.

"Actually," said Letitia, "Connie and I never got farther than the beginning of the hall which leads to the musicians' gallery. We met up with Sir Richard and he said he wished to speak with her for a moment." She added, innocent of the implication of her words, "I knew I was *de trop* so I left them to find Torrance."

Tessa's lips parted in dismay. "Did Sir Richard and Constance return to the ballroom too?" she asked urgently.

Letitia shrugged, unconcerned. "I didn't see them, but I suppose they may have by now."

Tessa began to believe that her recently faded fears for a social disaster occurring during the ball were about to be realized. She pulled her sister farther away from the others, and, oblivious of Letitia's protests, said in a low hiss, "Did they go on to the anterooms? Did you see them go into one of them?"

"I am sure I have no idea what they did," Letitia said impatiently.

"Letty, how could you be such a paperskull?" Tessa said angrily. "That wretched woman arranged this so she could be alone with Sir Richard without comment. How could you be so stupid as to let yourself be used in such a way?"

"It was no such thing," Letitia snapped. "What does it matter anyway? It is no concern of yours."

"Seeing that we are not tossed into the brink of a scandal is certainly a concern of mine," Tessa said heatedly. "Assuming that Constance was innocently engaged with you, I sent Hartfield to her when he came to find her a while ago."

At last she had Letitia's full attention. "Oh! But Constance wouldn't . . . Surely Lord Hartfield would not make a scene? Mamma says that gentlemen abhor them above all things. And he does not *truly* care, does he?"

"I have no idea what Hartfield will find, or what he will do," Tessa said with asperity, "but even if he cannot abide his wife, there is bound to be some unpleasantness."

"What can we do?" asked a wide-eyed Letitia as visions of a horrendous scene that would make her ball notorious rather than memorable assailed her.

"Probably nothing. It is a time since I sent Hartfield to find his wife. Whatever has happened is probably played out by now."

"But, Tess, you must do something," Letitia said, grabbing at her sister's arm. If there is a great fuss, my ball will be ruined."

The infamous phrase "I told you so" was on the tip of Tessa's tongue, but she virtuously refrained from uttering it. Instead she simply pursed her lips and nodded agreement. Though she doubted her ability to help the situation, she knew she had to try.

Tessa threaded her way through the crowded ballroom, acknowledging greetings but allowing no one to impede her way. She moved with a deliberate want of haste so as to attract no attention, but this made the ballroom seem twice its usual length, and when she reached the musicians' gallery and left the room the corridor of anterooms looked endless. There were four doors, but supposing that anyone bent on amorous intrigue would wish to be as far from the company as possible, she went without hesitation to the door at the end of the hall. Before she could reach it, it opened and Sir Richard came out and passed her sightlessly, his expression tight and his face noticeably pale. Tessa's last hopes sank. She bit at her lips, aware that her heart had begun to beat fast at the sight of Sir Richard, and felt that this was a foretoken of catastrophe come at last.

She glanced at the door and saw that Sir Richard had not completely closed it as he left. With the thud of her pulse in her ears she pressed herself against the wall next to it and stood very still until the voices in the room became distinct.

"You have no lures or enticements, Connie," Hartfield was saying scornfully. "They are wasted on me. The curtain has come down on our farce; you may as well accept it and take your bows gracefully. If you can."

"Even if you do have cause to be upset," Constance conceded, scorn in her tone as well, "you know as well as I that by tomorrow you will not think of this in the same way. By then your head will again control you instead of your pride. Do you know, Jon," she added matter-of-factly, "you are too much a mixture of hot blood and cold blood with very little that is more moderate. I think we should have dealt better if your character were more even."

"There was never any hope of our dealing together, Constance. The problem is that we didn't realize it until it was too late."

"Are you complaining, Jon?" she asked sweetly, and then laughed jeeringly. "I would have said that you had gotten out of our marriage exactly what you wished. It is only now, when it is my turn to demand payment of you, that you claim the price is too high. Name your price if you haven't enough of me already. You can have Caster Priory, if that is what it takes. Papa will agree to anything if I insist. In exchange I want absolutely nothing of you but your name."

"No, Connie," Hartfield said firmly and without heat. "I've let you cuckold me, not out of complaisance, but because there frankly is *nothing* I want of you. It is not that I am happy with my bargain, it is simply that I don't give a damn."

"Then why should you be so disobliging?"

"Disobliging?" he said on a note of surprise. "Is that how you term it? Not even the freedom to please myself in the same way or the comfort of living on your fortune would seem to me a fair exchange for what you wish."

"Do you know what manner of figure you will cut if this becomes known? And it surely will if you insist on making a scandal!" she asked scathingly.

"I care nothing for the opinions of the world. They have already seen fit to label me a fortune hunter; now they may shake their heads and call me a dupe or a fool, with my blessing," he said with cool bitterness. "What matters is what I think of myself, and not even your father has enough money to persuade me to swallow Cassidy's by-blow as my heir."

Tessa caught her breath so sharply at these words that she feared she had been heard by the occupants of the room. She had not meant to eavesdrop, only to see if an argument was in progress and to do what she could to prevent its becoming public. She had certainly never wished to hear their private business. But now she was frankly fascinated. She took a daring step closer to see better into the room, and saw Lord and Lady Hartfield standing near the mantel, their very stances making it clear that two strong wills had met and each was determined to prevail.

"I don't believe you, Jon," Constance said, but the assurance was no longer in her voice. "You are just venting your hurt pride and anger at me to assuage your vanity. If it is over with us, so is it over with your life at Gillane and any hope of ever possessing Caster Priory again. Those things mean more to you than I ever have, so you had best think carefully. Fortune hunters, I am told, must take things as they find them."

Hartfield did not answer her; after staring at her for a moment, he simply turned and began to leave the room.

Tessa, fearful of discovery in her compromising position, shrank into the far corner of the hall, knowing that she would not escape the hall in time and hoping thus to go unnoticed.

"You will not dare!" Constance's voice cried out clearly into the hall. "If you leave me, you will have nothing. I'll *see* to it that you never have anything again."

"I have nothing now," Jonathan said, obviously near to the door.

"You *can't* do this to me. I shall be ruined, destroyed."

"And if I let you do this to me, I shall be destroyed," he countered with a calmness that was a marked contrast to her rising hysteria. "The instinct for survival," he added, now with bitterness, "even emotional survival, is stronger than my desire for comfort. Do your worst, Connie, if you can. I truly don't give a damn."

"You might as well kill me, Jon," Constance said on a sob. "Feed me poison and be done with it. I think it might even be kinder."

"To which of us?" he responded sardonically. "Do you think this mess will be pleasant for me? Have no reflection on me? Don't tempt me with easy solutions."

Constance gave a high-pitched but muffled cry, and there was the sound of a scuffle. Tessa, who had once again allowed herself to be caught up in this tawdry little drama, felt the thud of her heart in her breast and in a sudden flight of imagination envisioned the marquis throttling his wife then and there. Without thought, instinctually, she moved out of her corner toward the room, and exactly as she did so, the door was flung open and Lord Hartfield came out of the room.

He might not have noticed her if she had remained still, but even as he turned to leave the room, he caught her motion and checked his own. Their eyes met, his containing a blazing anger she never would have guessed at from the calm, controlled sound of his voice, and which made her involuntarily shrink back from him. Then, as if she were invisible after all, he brushed past her and continued down the hall, also pushing past a startled waiter who had just come into the hall from the ballroom.

Tessa hesitated where she stood, not certain whether to return to the ballroom at once, which was her inclination, or to remain to see that Lady Hartfield was well. While she did not expect to find Constance murdered on the Turkey carpet, she had recognized the incipient hysteria in her voice and knew that the danger of a scene was not yet over. A choked cry that was nearly a wail coming from the room firmly decided her.

The waiter who had entered the hall as Lord Hartfield had left it was just closing the door of one of the other rooms, his tray now empty. There was another, louder cry from the room, and he stopped in his tracks, his eyes frankly questioning Tessa.

Acting on the first thought that came into her head, Tessa motioned to the waiter. He was not one of the Bellamy servants, but one of those sent by an agency to assist the regular staff for the evening. He came over to Tessa, boldly craning his neck to see who was weeping so, and was called sharply to order by Tessa, who told him to discover which of the guests was Lady Margaret Caster and to bring her at once to this room. To allay some of his curiosity, which she could see was rampant, she told him that Lady Margaret's sister had been taken suddenly ill. Then, with a curt nod of dismissal—for it would only make him wonder if she were too familiar—she turned her back on him and went into the room herself, firmly shutting the door.

Constance had cast herself on a convenient sofa and was sobbing wildly into its cushions, which mercifully muffled her cries. Not having her reticule about her, Tessa was without a vinaigrette, but she knew from having dealt with attacks of the vapours in her sister that sometimes merely a comforting presence or an ear to hear its causes was sufficient, so swallowing a sudden uprising of distaste, she sat beside Constance and laid a comforting hand on her heaving shoulder.

Constance could have no idea who was with her, for her face remained buried, but her weeping did become less violent and her wails were reduced to mere gasping sobs. After a few more minutes she raised herself up and Tessa moved a little away. She was acutely uncomfortable in her role of comforter, and she lifted up a silent prayer that the waiter would soon find someone to point out Lady Margaret to him and relieve her of this unwanted chore.

A faint look of puzzlement crossed Constance's face when she saw Tessa, but her upset was greater than her curiosity, and she began to speak without questioning Tessa's presence. "He can't do it," she said, mostly to herself between gulps of air. "I won't let him. Papa won't let him. How could Richard abandon me? How can Jon be so unfeeling?" She broke into heaving sobs again.

Tessa would never have thought that she would feel pity for the cosseted and spoiled daughter of the Duke of Gillane, but the incoherent, wild-eyed creature who suddenly grasped her hands for support and began whispering wild things about death and ruin, shivering with the force of her emotions, was pathetic.

Such complete loss of control was alien to the not easily ruffled temperament of Tessa. When matters had come to a step beyond dreadful, it seemed to her, it was the time to pull oneself together, call on one's resources, and do what one could to bring matters right again. She thought it nothing short of foolish to add to one's distress by indulging in an excess of grief, but in fairness to the wretched woman beside her, she admitted that a state of such complete unhappiness had mercifully never yet come her way.

But if Tessa could feel pity for Constance, she could feel no sympathy. Whatever manner of husband Jonathan Hartfield had been, Constance had chosen her own course and if her illicit liaison with Sir Richard had brought her to this, where else was the blame to be laid?

Tessa had not been looking at Constance, but beyond her, and turning her eyes back to her charge, she was disconcerted to find Constance staring at her with unblinking red-rimmed eyes. "You don't like me, do you?" Constance said with sudden lucidity. "Why are you here?"

This was so unanswerable that Tessa flushed. At that moment, to her undisguised relief, the door opened and Lady Margaret came into the room. Margaret took in the scene and gauged the situation with reasonable accuracy at once. She raised her eyebrows at finding Tessa with her sister-in-law, but made no comment.

It was Tessa who spoke. "I am sorry to trouble you, Meg," she said, rising with alacrity and edging toward the door. "Constance had a disagreement with Jonathan and became distraught," she added, hating herself for the euphemisms but fearful that a more detailed explanation would mean further involvement. Constance could say what she wished to Margaret; it was in any case not Tessa's story to tell. Tessa felt guilty for even knowing of Constance's disgrace, because she had come by her information so underhandedly, and to have divulged it to anyone at all must be dishonorable.

Lady Margaret gave her friend a brief understanding smile. "Of course it is no trouble. You had best return to your guests," Margaret advised her. "Mr. McAffe has already remarked on your absence. He fears you have forgotten your promise to go in with him to supper."

Tessa gratefully seized upon this suggestion and made good her escape, leaving her least-wanted and most-troublesome guest to the capable hands of her friend.

Chapter Two

Jonathan Hartfield took another pacing turn about the morning room of his mother's house. The only other occupant of the room was his sister Margaret, and except for an occasional worried glance cast in his direction, she was giving her full attention to her needlework, leaving him to the silence he obviously preferred.

Jonathan had an orderly mind and was not generally given to indecision. A number of weighty problems presently confronted him, and in these he knew his mind. The concern which troubled him now was relatively minor, and it vexed him all the more that he could not be certain of the best course to take.

This matter was, in fact, a person, Tessa Bellamy; or rather, the knowledge that he was reasonably convinced she possessed. He did not know why or how she had come to be outside the anteroom where he had left his wife the evening before last, but the moment their eyes had met, he had had the impression that she knew every private word that had passed between him and Constance.

Soon enough, his wife's name and his own would be dragged through the mud, the byword of every lordling and kitchen maid. Given the tarnish put upon his name by his father's gaming and debts and his own reputation as a gazetted fortune hunter, one more disgrace might have hardly seemed to matter, but it did to him, and the inevitability of it made it no easier to bear. Some of the worst of it was the knowledge that his own indifference had played a part in bringing him to this unsavory pass. He was not even certain that he cared for himself, but for his mother and his yet-unmarried sister he cared deeply. He would come about; he knew from experience that he always did, but the scandal would shatter his overly sensitive mother and would place a stain even upon the utterly blameless Margaret that might well destroy what chances were left to her of a decent marriage.

But even if the inevitable could only be delayed, he wanted that time. He would be able to put his own affairs in order and do what he could to prepare his family for the grief about to fall upon them. If the viper tongues of the gossips should spread even a hint of his dishonor now, it would not need the prepared Crim. Con. action or the bill of divorcement to make himself and all connected with him infamous overnight.

One course of action open to him was to do absolutely nothing. Though his acquaintance with Miss Bellamy was not great, she had struck him favorably in the few times they had met, and most particularly last night, when he had been quite surprised by both her candour and her attractiveness. He had, like most people, been wont to consider her the plain sister, but realized that it was only in the comparison that she suffered; Tessa Bellamy was quite lovely in her own right. She also seemed to him to have something of her father's character about her and he knew Sir Edwin well, both as his father's friend, and as a kind adviser at the time of the marquis' death. Sir Edwin was a man of sense and discretion, and it might be hoped that some of this quality had been passed on to his offspring.

But an even briefer acquaintance with the younger girl, Letitia, made it clear that this could not be counted on, for he judged her to be self-centered, ambitious, and probably not to be trusted with any secret that it was not in her own best interest to keep. Good blood, he had reason to know, was not necessarily a guarantee of character.

Even as he thought this of Letitia Bellamy, he smiled ruefully. In justice, he was forced to admit that his opinion of her was decidedly biased. He was inclined to paint spoiled young beauties in his own wife's image, and there were few who would benefit from this drawing.

Margaret had told him in her quiet way that Tessa had summoned her to deal with Constance's hysteria, but from her naive questions he knew that if Tessa knew, she had not confided it in his sister. There was, of course, the possibility that it was only his own imagination that made him feel Tessa was cognizant of his difficulties. She might have appeared outside the door at the very moment of their meeting and be as ignorant as his own sister obviously was.

Then why, he demanded of himself as he stared out onto the prospect of the mist-enshrouded garden, could he not be comfortable simply letting the matter lie? There was no answer within himself. He only knew that he felt nearly compelled to act on the other course open to him, that of calling upon Tessa and discovering the extent of her knowledge and what she meant to do with it.

Simply bringing the matter into a conversation with her would be uncomfortable and delicate; finding an excuse to speak with her alone when their acquaintance was so slight seemed nearly impossible. There was even the danger that if she did not know as much as he suspected, her quick mind would guess at the whole, or already knowing it, would realize the power her knowledge gave her over him.

But he knew what he must do, for his own peace if no other reason, and dismissing all further argument and doubt from his mind, he applied himself to the problems of carrying the thing off.

When the Marquis of Hartfield's card was brought up to her in the back parlour which the Bellamy ladies used to perform their domestic tasks, Tessa was plainly surprised. "Did he ask for me, Winthrop," she asked the butler, who had carried the bit of pasteboard himself, "or is it just that I am the only one at home?"

"He asked for you, miss."

Tessa was engaged in the homey task of mending flounces on petticoats, and was dressed accordingly in a plain cotton round gown, her hair, cut short in the careless curls and waves made fashionable by the dashing Lady Caroline Lamb, making her look as wild and distracted as that ethereal beauty. She had no intention of going out, had expected no callers, and had not so much as brushed rice powder on her face to give her complexion a fashionable pallor.

She might have refused to receive him, of course; as she was the only member of the family at home, it would even have been the proper thing for her to do, but curiosity and perhaps something a bit more made her wishful to see him. Still, although she was not a vain woman, and did not generally care that her friends might find her looking less than her best when they called, for an indefinable reason it bothered her that Hartfield should find her in such a state.

But she had to decide at once whether her vanity or her curiosity mattered more to her, and with only a small vexed exclamation, she decided on the latter. "Please send him to me, Winthrop," she instructed, and as soon as the butler had gone, she raced about the room shoving petticoats into the workbasket and digging out a less-intimate piece of linen to work upon. She gathered together the scattered pattern cards she and Letitia had been perusing earlier and finally made a quick trip to the looking glass above the mantel to see if a bit of patting might make the negligence of her coiffure seem more deliberate than accidental.

Tessa heard his footsteps approaching in the hall and resumed her chair, so that when he entered the room there was nothing about her appearance to tell him that her heart was racing from her exertions or that any other thing ruffled the cool exterior of the young woman who held out her hand to him.

As he entered the room, their eyes met, much as they had in the anteroom hallway two nights ago. There was an instant and silent understanding between them and he knew his instincts had not betrayed him. The young woman who, despite her unfashionable dishabille, faced him with cool confidence, with no trace of simpering coyness or an arch knowingness, could be dealt with straightforwardly and intelligently. He abandoned at once all plans of subterfuge or roundaboutation and decided to speak to her with a bit of her own outspokenness. "Thank you for seeing me, Miss Bellamy," he said. "My luck is in to have found you at home and alone. But I see that I interrupt you."

The corners of Tessa's mouth lifted in a slightly sardonic but nevertheless attractive smile. "Is that your way of telling me I look a quiz, my lord? I am afraid you must take me as you find me, for with Mama and Letty out shopping for Letty's bride clothes, I didn't think to have any visitors this morning."

"Or wish for any?" he said, returning her smile. "Then I must be honored that you have received me. To be honest," he added candidly, "I am grateful that you have and that I find you this way, for I'd supposed the only way I would see you would be in the company of your mother or sister, and I'd have the difficult task of finding a way to speak with you alone."

Tessa sat down on a small sofa near the windows that overlooked the garden, and indicated a chair across from her to him. "You surprise me, my lord," she said in a voice that sounded more matter-of-fact than startled. "Why should you wish to see me alone? Your object cannot be dalliance," she added, again with the quick smile that he found alluring, "for I am not the sort of female to attract that sort of thing, unless you supposed my sister Letty to be the elder and have mistakenly asked for me. But if that is so, I must say I admire your aplomb, for you did not look the least chagrined when you came into the room and discovered that 'Miss Bellamy' was not the vision of loveliness of several nights ago."

He saw by the laughter in her eyes that she was quizzing him, but as he regarded her, he became increasingly aware that she stirred in him an unexpected response. Dalliance was certainly not his object, but he would not at all have minded indulging in this pursuit, and only the importance of his mission and the fact that this young woman before him was the daughter of a man who had stood a friend to him prevented him from the falling into it.

But though her words were teasing, he read in them a self-defamation that he could not allow to stand. "You do yourself injustice, Miss Bellamy. I won't offer you the Spanish coin of telling you that you are more beautiful than your sister, but not every man prefers a pair of speaking eyes to a lively, intelligent mind, and when this is coupled with a face and form that possess an exquisiteness of their own, the combination is far more irresistible than a mere outward beauty."

"Are you speaking for yourself, my lord?" she

asked without archness. "If you are, I must thank you, for that is quite the prettiest compliment that I have received in a very long time. I only wish my present appearance was deserving of it."

"Your appearance must always be worthy of compliment," he said in a soft, almost caressing voice which made Tessa raise her brows.

"Ah. Then dalliance *is* your object?" she said coolly.

He shook his head and smiled. "No." Though he had come to her feeling more driven than desirous of doing so, he was now glad that he had. His anxieties about Tessa's character had vanished and were replaced with an opinion of her that was more than merely favorable for his present needs. A thought flashed into his mind, to be banished again; there were some avenues that were forever closed to him, whatever his future might hold.

This thought had a purpose, though. It brought him up short, recalling to him what he must do. "I have a private matter to discuss with you. I think you know what it is." To his surprise, he saw that he had discomfited her. Two small spots of color came to her cheeks.

"I won't pretend I do not," she admitted, "but I must first beg your pardon. I had no original intention of deliberately eavesdropping. It is not important how I came to be there, but when I realized the argument that was in progress, the truth is that I was fascinated by what was none of my concern, and I listened." Her eyes had been lowered for this speech, but now she raised them again to him. "I've been half-expecting you, you know, and half-dreading it. I'd almost convinced myself that you would arrive the very next morning breathing fire and threatening dire consequences if I repeated what I'd heard to a soul."

"Is that your reading of my character?" he asked with a faint mocking surprise. "Be more discriminating in your sources; I am not so great an ogre."

"Nor am I usually given to such fancy," Tessa said lightly. "But on the other hand, I would have regarded it as fantastical indeed to imagine that you would come paying me compliments."

"That was not intentional, but inevitable," he said gallantly, but with sincerity.

A faint rosiness was again visible in Tessa's cheeks, but this time it was not embarrassment. "You need have no fear that I shall ever speak of it to anyone," she said brusquely to hide her confusion. "I would consider myself sunk beneath reproach were I to be guilty of spreading a story that I had no business knowing in the first place and had come by so shabbily."

"Then I must thank you, Miss Bellamy, and inform you that I am in your debt," he said formally. "There are those, I know, who would consider my difficulties a delicious tidbit to be shared with their friends."

"Was that your reading of my character?"

"No, not really. You do not dissemble; it must follow that you do not carry tales. I wish my own character might be so commendable." The words were complimentary, the soft expression in his eyes even more so.

Though Tessa was generally cast into the shade by Letitia, she was not uncourted and was often the recipient of the most fulsome compliments. Never did she behave in what she condemned as an absurdly missish manner. She could not control her coloring, but she could school her features, and she regarded him now with what she hoped was no more than amused interest. "Oh, I am a pattern card for virtue," she said amiably, and then added with her usual candour, "I know it is impertinent of me to ask this, but since you have brought the thing up, and I am however unwillingly and unwantedly involved, I should like to know what you mean to do now?"

This was not something he was prepared to discuss with anyone. "What does one do in an impossible situation?" he said with a perceptible distance in
his tone. "One does what is necessary and makes
the best of things."

Tessa's preference for plain speaking was not a
euphemism for insensitivity, and she felt chagrined
that she had allowed the intimacy of their banter to
betray her into going too far. "No doubt that is the
best course," she said levelly. "You know you may
rely on my discretion."

He rose to take his leave of her. "Thank you, Miss
Bellamy. I don't tease myself that this disgrace can
be averted from my name, but the time that your
silence gives me to prepare myself for the onslaught
of gossip will be invaluable and is appreciated." He
took the hand she held out to him and bowed over
it.

"There is nothing to thank me for," Tessa replied,
feeling let down that he was leaving her, and with
the formality of a stranger, which she had for a
moment nearly forgotten he was. "I do this more for
my honor than for yours."

And when he was gone a few minutes later, and
Tessa was again sitting with a petticoat in her lap,
she became conscious of a deep sense of regret. She
did not remain unwed for a want of offers, and
certainly not all of those had been from men who
would have wed her dowry rather than her person.
She might at this very moment have been a wealthy
countess if she had chosen to accept one of her
suitors. Her simple reason for remaining in the single state was that she had yet to be tempted to
change it.

Tessa did not regard herself as at all romantical,
but neither did she wish for a cold-blooded marriage
of convenience. She did not yearn for a grand passion to leave her unsure of whether she was on her
head or her heels, but regarded strong mutual

attraction, and a sameness of thought that would make her and her husband firm friends, as an unnegotiable term in a marriage she contracted.

So far she had yet to meet a man in whom reposed both of her criteria, or rather, she had not known that she had met him before today. If she was not in the habit of dissembling to others, neither would she do so to herself, and she knew that in Jonathan Hartfield her search was met with success. It was disconcerting and dispiriting to know that that one man was unattainable, but not being at all the sort of female who develops *tendres* and languishes after an unrequited love, she decided simply to put him out of her mind.

But by midday the next day, the name of Jonathan Hartfield and that of his wife were on the lips of every member of the ton who had come up to town for the short season before retiring to their family seats for the holidays. For the better part of the day, Tessa was one of the few people to remain in ignorance of the events leading to this. Shopping and gossipy visits were not particularly to her taste, and she had spent another quiet morning on her own while the rest of her family was abroad.

It was nearly two when she heard her father, who generally spent his mornings at his chambers, come in, and a bit after that when she heard her mother admonishing a servant in the hall. Tessa laid aside the chair cover she was embroidering and began to gather up her silks. When Lady Frances had returned home yesterday and learned that Lord Hartfield had called and been received by her elder daughter, Tessa had been sternly rebuked, not for receiving Hartfield without a chaperon, but for doing so dressed, as she called it, like a ragamuffin.

Tessa was clad in a similar style today, but she did not care to endure another of her mother's lectures, and had intended to slip into her room to change before going down for luncheon. She was not quick enough, however, and had only just risen from her chair when her mother came into the room.

"If you are coming down for luncheon, Tess," Lady Frances said, and it was a comment and not a reproach, "you had best change and be quick about it. Torrance lunches with us and he and Letty must then be off at once to visit his sister at Richmond. They dine there as well, so it shall just be you and I tonight for the Ponsonbys' card party. Papa has his own engagement, the Daffy Club, I believe."

Tess did as she was told and changed quickly to a spotted muslin that was more suited to visitors, but even so, the rest of the family were already at table when she came into the dining room. She slid into her place as unobtrusively as possible, but still gained a small frown from her mother, which was somewhat mitigated by the warm smile she received from her father.

She began at once to eat the consommé that was already cooling, as she listened idly to the chatter of her sister to her betrothed.

"I nearly swooned in the middle of Madame Celeste's when Lucy Brecker came in and told me the news, did I not, Mamma?" Letitia said, rolling her eyes dramatically. "I have ever been too sensitive, and when Lucy spoke to me, it was all I could do to murmur, 'Not my dear Constance.' Then, of course, I said I could not believe it. Well, it is still impossible to credit, but it must be true, for *everyone* is speaking of it."

"You certainly are," Sir Edwin said dryly. "I have heard nothing else since we sat down. This is too serious a matter, touching the lives of people who are our friends, for us to indulge in idle gossip." Though his tone was stern, his daughters were too well acquainted with his easy nature for Letitia to pay him much heed.

"But you do not know of it, do you, Tess?" Letitia

said eagerly, seeing the puzzlement in her sister's expression and sensing a new direction in which she might impart her information.

"Other than that it obviously concerns your friend Constance Hartfield and is, as might be expected, unsavory, no, I do not," Tessa responded with an indifference she was far from feeling.

"Oh, Tess, it is the most dreadful thing," Letitia said, sounding more excited than abashed. "Connie was found dead this morning by her dresser. Can you imagine it?"

"No," said Tessa feelingly, as a sudden knot formed in her stomach. "How could it happen?"

"You must have noticed that Constance has scarcely been seen in the sennight since my ball?" Tessa shook her head. "In any event," Letitia went on, "she has not been, and Caroline Fischer, who is her cousin on her mother's side, called to see if she were ill and has told everyone that she has never seen anyone looking so hagged! Caro said that if she had been in some other house she would not even have recognized Connie, and Connie told her that she had been suffering the migraine and had had trouble sleeping, which accounted for it, and only think, that was the very thing that brought her to her end. Who would have thought it?"

"Probably not your sister," Sir Edwin interjected exasperatedly. "If she made sense of that speech, I can only say her understanding is superior to mine."

Letitia gave her father a pert smile and then said to her sister in the careful accents one might use to a dim-witted child, "Constance was taking laudanum to help her sleep and to ease the pain of her migraine, and last night she mistook the dose and is this morning dead of her own hand, though accidentally, of course. You *must* be the very last person in town to hear of it," she added, as if this proved Tessa's thickness. "Madame Celeste's was abuzz with the news by the time Mamma and I left, which was not

long afterward, I can tell you. I was *that* overset."
This last was exclusively for Lord Torrance. "My
poor sensibilities are so easily disordered. You must
learn to be patient with me, Walter."

Letitia's last words on Constance's misadventure
had the effect of relaxing Tessa's unexpected tension.
Unbidden, at the news of Constance's death, the
words had come to her: "What does one do in an
impossible situation?" and though the thought after
this had not been completely formed, the outline of
its ugliness was clear in her mind. She could not say
what she had expected to hear, but to learn that
Constance had died by mistaking the amount of her
sleeping draught was more relieving than surprising.

A motion from Sir Edwin brought the hovering
footman to remove the first course. "No doubt Torrance shall learn to be as forbearing as the others
who love you," he said dryly to his younger daughter.
"I think, though, that it would behoove us to discuss this unhappy event as little as possible outside
our own family circle. I am sure we all count the
Caster family as friends, and this must be regarded
as a tragedy to them and particularly to the Duke
of Gillane, who, I understand, was very attached to
his daughter. It will not do for us to bandy about
their misfortune as if it were only the latest bit of
scandal."

Letitia, who though far from unintelligent, did
not possess the great sensibility that she imagined,
needed a much more direct rebuke than this. She
regarded her friendship with the unfortunate Lady
Hartfield and the Caster family as license to discuss
their difficulties more completely than anyone else.
Sir Edwin understood this, but he hoped she would
take the gentler hint in front of her betrothed and
not so expose herself. It was a vain hope, but also a
vain concern. Even Letitia's imperfections were virtues in the eyes of the besotted viscount.

"I assure you, Papa," she said with no trace of

having understood him, "no one will talk of anything else for *weeks*. Almost I wish we were to go to
the Ponsonbys' party tonight after all. You must
listen to every word that is said, Tess," she instructed her sister, "and tell me the whole, especially if there is anything said of its not truly being
an accident."

"What do you mean?" Tessa asked so sharply that
every head turned to her. "What else could it be?"
she said more moderately.

Aware from the frown her husband cast her that
his displeasure in this continuing conversation was
growing, Lady Frances intervened strongly enough
for the conversation to at last be turned.

Tessa in general agreed with her father that Letitia's
penchant for idle gossip and scandal was to be
deplored, and if possible, curbed, but for once she
wished nothing more than to listen to her sister's
chatter. To further frustrate her, almost the moment
luncheon was over, Letitia ran to her room to change
for her journey, and Lady Frances tagged her elder
daughter to entertain Lord Torrance. Sir Edwin had
quickly escaped to his study with the excuse of work,
and Lady Frances, at least in privacy with her
husband, admitted that though she was glad of the
match with Torrance and was pleased by his obvious
attachment to her dear Letty, she could wish that his
virtues included conversability.

Tessa obediently kept up a steady stream of incon-
sequential conversation that required little response
from his lordship, but beneath the surface she fret-
ted for an excuse to run upstairs for a word with
Letitia before she could leave. Letitia's suggestion
that Constance had not died accidentally after all
might have been nothing more than her own drama-
tization, but Tessa was again aware of an unpleasant
tightness about her stomach.

At last Lady Frances mentioned that Letitia was
taking a great deal of time, and Tessa seized on the

excuse of discovering the cause. Before her mother
could raise any objection, she was already gone from
the room.

Mary Perkins, the abigail whom the girls shared,
was fastening a pearl bracelet on her mistress's arm,
and Letitia was gathering up with her free hand her
gloves and reticule when Tessa came into the dressing room. Tessa had her own dressing room, joined
to the bedchamber she had removed to nearly a year
ago, wanting to be more to the back of the house.

"I suppose Mamma has sent you to hurry me,"
Letitia said when she saw her sister. "Well, I am
ready. I could not decide between the blue sarcenet
and the lemon muslin." She had chosen the former
and now pirouetted before her sister. "Will this do,
do you think?"

"Perfectly," Tessa said shortly. "I wish to speak
with you for a moment before you go. Please leave
us, Mary."

A slight impatient frown marred Letitia's perfect
features, but when Tessa made it clear it concerned
the recent misfortune of her friend, it vanished. She
did not intend, though, to give her sister the information she wished without cost. "It sometimes
amazes me," she said condescendingly, "how it can
be that someone who has been out for three whole
seasons can be so naive." It gave Letitia a decided
sense of superiority to know that after three seasons,
Tessa was still, in her estimation, on the shelf, while
she herself in one brief, triumphant season had
snagged an eligible *parti* deemed by most a "catch."
The thought of being a married woman, with the
precedence that would give her over the older Tessa,
was a boost to her vanity.

Letitia, never known for her subtlety, seldom
missed the opportunity of patronizing Tessa now
that she felt in a position of superiority. "Though if
you will spend all your time at home looking like a
quiz, it isn't wonderful that you never know what is

happening in the world. If you don't have a care, dear, you shall end up a veritable ape leader and not my best efforts nor Mamma's will ever find a husband for you."

Tessa kept admirable control on her rising temper. "What has this to do with Constance?"

"Why, nothing," Letitia admitted. "But *everyone* knows that Sir Richard was Constance's grand passion. If Hartfield came to town so unexpectedly, it must be that he meant for her to give him up. Why else could it be that she retired from society nearly at once and Caro found her looking so hagged?" As if coming to a sudden decision, she caught at her sister's arm and drew her close, an unnecessary bit of melodrama, for they were quite alone. "Did you know that Sir Richard, too, has not been in company since my ball? He has *said* that he is having tenant difficulties on his estates in Ireland, but it is believed that Constance flew to his protection when Hartfield made his demands on her and Sir Richard refused to elope, sending her back to her husband, preferring to go into retirement on his estates rather than discover himself saddled with a ruined woman. Poor Connie!" But if she felt grief for her wretched friend, there was no sign of it in her sparkling eyes.

If Tessa knew anything of the matter from the expression she had seen on Sir Richard's face the night of Letitia's ball, he had been halfway to Ireland by sunup. But there was enough truth in the assumption that the Hartfields' marriage had come to pieces to make her uneasy. "Who is saying such a thing?" she demanded. "It had better be Constance's own coachman who took her to Sir Richard and back again to her husband; any less sure source would make such gossip unconscionable. "I hope *you* do not mean to tell this to anyone else. Papa is right, we owe it to our friends not to add to their grief."

"Oh, you are so prosy, Tess," Letita said impatiently, picking up her reticule again. "If you are so concerned for the family, why don't you go to your friend Meg, who is as tiresomely pious as you are. No doubt she will like somebody to tell her that her brother is a pattern card of virtue and his marriage to Constance a tribute to love matches. I, however, have an appointment to keep in the *real* world."

That one portion at least of Letitia's advice was sound, and returning downstairs, Tessa at once sent a note to her friend. She did not care to call in person, for in times of upset even the closest friends could be *de trop*. Tessa simply wrote her condolences and made it clear that Lady Margaret might call upon her in any capacity.

It was not until the day after next that Tessa heard from her friend. Unsurprised, she assumed that Margaret was having her hands full seeing to her mother, who would be bound to take this news as though a mortal blow had been delivered to her.

When Tessa arrived next door in answer to Margaret's summons, the latter confirmed this. "We have been at sixes and sevens, Tess, or you know I should have sent for you sooner. You are so good, I know you would have come to me even in the midst of this mess, but it would not be fair of me to place the burdens of my family on your shoulders. We have had to have Dr. Omney for Mamma, who is so distraught that she has taken to her bed. And poor Jon, he is so silent and grim, and though Mamma means well, it does not help at all to constantly remind him that Constance has had a blessed release from her unhappy situation. Which is absurd of course! Who would not rather be a partner in an unhappy marriage than dead?" She sighed and added confidentially, "But it is true that one does not know whether to condole or congratulate Jon, and though I know it is a dreadful thing to say, it is certainly a release for him. But of course, he is wretched, with all of Mamma's weepings, the duke's ravings that it is Jon's fault that Connie came to this, and the unforgivably viperish gossip." She cast a sidelong glance at Tess. "I suppose you have heard the talk that is going about?"

Tessa had indeed. It was everything that Letitia had told to her and more. The easy prediction that Constance's death would be a sensation to surpass the time that Caroline Lamb was said to have attempted to slash her wrists publicly for love of Lord Byron was quite correct. Discussion of Constance's affair with Sir Richard was open and the assumption that this beauty had done herself in for unrequited love was rampant. It was not likely that there would be any cessation of the talk only a few days after the event, but the Duke of Gillane, who it was reported was grief-stricken to the point of nearly being out of his senses, was adding fuel to the scandal by telling anyone who would listen that the full blame for it all might be found in Hartfield. He was blamed not only of her demise but also for the failure of their marriage, which he claimed had led to that.

But it was not enough for the duke to malign Jonathan publicly. Margaret confirmed a story Tessa had heard that the duke had, in front of his servants, cast Jonathan's belongings from his house, and had Jonathan been present, would have likely had him removed bodily as well.

"Which was most deliberate and unnecessary," said Margaret censoriously. "Jonathan had been staying more here than there in any case, and after Connie died, had only remained at Gillane House for appearance' sake, intending to remove his things the moment the funeral was ended. I have heard that the duke even tried to prevent Jon from attending that, but Jon won't speak of it to me or Mama or anyone, so I don't know if it is true or not."

Added to this unhappy information was the verifiable fact that the duke had removed every last penny from the account that he had set up for his daughter and son-in-law at Drummond's, though some of it had belonged to Jonathan through the annuity which was all that was left to him of his own inheritance. The dowager had declared all her faculties suspended at this news. It was an evil fate, she had declared, that their return to comfort after her husband's death should again be torn from them so that they might again be expected to be cast into the street hourly. This of course was nonsense, as Margaret assured her friend, for Jonathan had wisely purchased the house in his mother's name out of the sum the duke had settled on him at his marriage, and as Jon had also purchased for them both annuities greater than his own so that they might always be provided for, it was not likely that beyond the abandonment of a few luxuries which the Hartfields had provided for them, their lives would materially change.

Socially it was quite another matter. The whole family was in black gloves, of course, and would not have gone out in the world in any event, but Margaret confessed to Tessa that at least in regard to her mother's insistence that they live as quietly as possible for the next few months, she was in entire agreement. It was excessively uncomfortable, after all, to walk into a room and have all conversation hush because what was being said could not continue in your presence.

Tessa did what she could to comfort her friend. But beyond soothing words and a veiled hint that should there be any want, Tessa would stand their friend, there was little she could offer of practical help. What she did do was give up much of her daytime activities and some of her evening engagements as well to spend time with the Caster ladies. It was no chore to be with Margaret, of course, but the dowager's company was decidedly taxing.

Tessa and her family were among the few of their

friends regularly received, so much of the time that Tess spent at the next house was *en famille* and was marked by an unrelieved gloom brought on by Lady Hartfield's penchant for melodrama. This, though, if not dispelled, was at the least lightened on the rare occasions when Jonathan would join them. He could usually manage to quiz, or if that failed, exasperate his mother out of her doldrums at least for a time.

Tessa rather marveled at Jonathan Hartfield. If ever a man was beset on all sides, it was he, yet though she might catch in his voice an occasional trace of sardonicism or bitterness, there was never self-pity or blame against those that wronged him, or even against the fickleness of fate.

At times when the dowager was especially vitriolic in her self-indulgent whinings and condemnation of her son, it was all Tessa could do to keep her tongue. More than once she plied her needle with unaccustomed ferocity to hold her peace, and glancing up when she dared, had found Hartfield watching her with a mixture of gratitude and amusement. It quickly became habit for them to seek each other's eyes as soon as his mother fell into one of her tirades, and the smile that Tessa saw in his eyes she came to know as an appreciation of her understanding.

Finally there was an afternoon when Tessa, taking luncheon with the family, let slip the guard on her speech. Her reproach to the dowager was mild enough, but that lady, so unused to receiving criticism of any sort in her own sphere, took umbrage and turned from her usual subject to castigate her guest instead, forgetting entirely as she did so all of Tessa's selfless kindness toward her and her children.

Immediately the meal was finished, the dowager claimed the headache as an excuse to retire to her room and insisted on the company of Lady Margaret, suggesting in quite a pointed way that Jonathan might see Tessa out. Margaret obediently left the room with her mother, casting Tessa a distracted and apologetic look, and Tessa found herself alone with Lord Hartfield.

He spoke at once. "I won't presume to apologize for my mother's rudeness, Miss Bellamy. I only beg you will understand the severe cares that have been thrust upon her of late and allow for any consequent aberration in her manner."

It was all Tessa could do to prevent herself from saying that it was her experience that the dowager was always selfish and inclined to be rude when checked, but she acknowledged her own wrong instead. "It was I who should not have spoken. I am afraid my wretched tongue betrayed me, my lord, and I beg your pardon." This was nicely said and would doubtless have ended the matter, but once again Tessa was a victim of her own honesty. "But I don't know how you can bear it," she added.

He gave her one of his half-smiles in which she detected a hint of sadness but, remarkably, absolutely no self-pity. "Mamma does not mean to be cruel. I don't think it occurs to her that her words might be hurtful."

In Tessa's opinion this made the dowager's behavior worse, but this time she managed to keep her thought to herself. "The Duke of Gillane means to hurt you, though," she said. "I won't insult you by pretending that we have neither of us heard the abominable things he has been saying of you. I think it completely unconscionable that he may do so with impunity, and all the more so since I was acquainted with Constance and know . . ." She stopped abruptly, and flushed slightly, not so much at what she had said as at what she had been about to say.

His tone and expression assured her that he had not this time taken offense at her implied judgment of his wife's behavior. "He does mean to be hurtful," the marquis admitted, "but in his way he is as little responsible for what he is doing as is Mamma. This is not so much him speaking as it is his grief. No matter what occurred, if Connie had lived or not, I must have found myself in the center of a storm. So you see, I was not unprepared for it and consequently find it easier to bear than you might think."

Tessa did not think that any manner of preparation would have enabled her to bear the verbal and emotional browbeating that Hartfield received with unflagging equanimity, but she could not trust herself to say more on the subject, and she let it subside.

As their acquaintance grew in these days, Tessa found her attraction and liking for him growing along with her admiration at his forbearance. At moments she managed to convince herself that his feelings were not dissimilar, but the truth was that if he did feel any regard for her, it was not apparent on the surface. He treated her in the same vein that he treated Lady Margaret: he was amiable, but faintly indifferent.

Her imaginings would not do, of course, and Tessa, who often declared that she hadn't a romantic bone in her body, decided that she was simply becoming caught up in the romance of his plight—as for that matter had Letitia, who had taken to calling on the Casters far more than had been her wont before Jonathan had come to live there. The same blood, after all, flowed in the veins of both sisters, and Tessa reasoned that if Letitia could show a consideration that was not a normal part of her character, by visiting with the dowager and Lady Margaret, then so might she give rein to qualities that were not a normal part of her own character. In any event, she did not regard the rather vague, indefinable sensations that his company could arouse in her as anything to give her concern and therefore did not allow it to make her anxious in the least.

As the short season drew to a close, and all the

first families of the ton who had come up to town began to drift to their own seats or to engagements at the estates of friends for the approaching holidays, the talk began to die a natural death. When Tessa and her family, who by choice did not have an estate of their own, prepared to leave for Boxwood, the home of her uncle the Earl of Dexter, where they had spent Christmas every year that Tessa could remember, an invitation was extended to the Caster family to join them, for the earl was an amiable man who welcomed all to his home with genuine pleasure.

Lady Margaret thanked her friend most earnestly for her thoughtfulness, but regretfully declined for herself, her mother, and her brother. "Jon intends to remain in the city, to brave this thing out," she confided. "I don't know what will be accomplished by deliberately setting his face against the talk and the slurs of the duke, but he says that he will stay in town and hold up his head to them all."

Tessa thought it cruel of him to insist on remaining when she did not doubt that Margaret and their mother would have been more than glad to have removed from town, to give them the freedom of something more than this house if for no other reason. Margaret admitted that she would have dearly wished to spend Christmas with her friend, but insisted that the decision to remain was entirely her own and her mother's and against the urgings of Jonathan, who did not expect them to maintain his stance. "For if we do not stand beside him," Margaret concluded, "who shall?"

This was unarguable, but Tessa at least gained a promise from Margaret to write frequently and to come at once to Boxwood, with or without notice, if remaining in town became unbearable.

By the end of the week the town was so thin of company that the Casters were not remarkable for their absence in society. The Bellamys, who had waited for some business of Sir Edwin's to conclude, were among the last of those to finally remove the knocker from the front door of their house and begin their journey along the much-traveled Great North Road.

Chapter Three

The journey and visit of the Bellamy family to the principal seat of the Earl of Dexter were remarkable only for being totally uneventful. Lord Torrance joined them just before Christmas, as expected, and Colin, who had planned to be in attendance on the archbishop, arrived within the same hour, unexpected but most welcome, especially to his cousin Tessa. She was finding the continuing fuss over her sister's approaching nuptials a bit wearing, particularly in light of Letitia's tendency to continuously remind one and all that though she was the younger, it was she who was to marry first.

Tessa had the happy knack of adapting herself with pleasure to her surroundings. When she was in the city she was very content to live there and felt no longing for a more rustic life; when in the country, she did not at all miss the bustle and pulse of the city, pleased to slow her pace to match that of her surroundings. Therefore she did not dwell a great deal on her life in town or the friends she had left behind there except to wonder from time to time how they were faring.

When she received her first letter from Lady Margaret, about a fortnight after her arrival at

Boxwood, she had no inkling that matters were not steadily improving for her friends as she had supposed they would when the gossip died away, for Lady Margaret's letter and those which followed contained conversational information and light gossip with only an occasional mention of her mother or brother and none at all of their difficulties.

Arrangements were made for the Bellamy ladies to travel with Lord Torrance on the Monday after Boxing Day to his family who lived in Pembrokeshire. Sir Edwin had politely declined the invitation, retreating to the convenience his profession offered for excuse. The tiresome company of his future son-in-law aside, *he* did not care for rustication, which was why his immense fortune had never purchased an estate appropriate to his station. He declared that he had family enough keeping up mouldering ruins for him to spend ten months of twelve communing with nature if he wished, and that was rustication enough for him.

Tessa was not looking forward to the proposed visit to Pembrokeshire. Between her sister's tiresome condescension and Lord Torrance's vapidness, the prospect of yet another month in their nearly exclusive company was not precisely attractive. In idle moments she tried to imagine an excuse which would allow her to either remain at Boxwood or return to town with her father, and that would neither give offense to Torrance or his family nor call upon her head her mother's wrath. The answer to her dilemma arrived in the post three days before they were set to leave.

Its appearance was innocent enough—a letter from Lady Margaret, franked as usual by her brother. The first page was unremarkable, containing only the usual inconsequentials. It was not until she turned to the next that she saw that the rest of the missive had been written in obvious haste, crossed and recrossed and blotched here and there by the application of copious amounts of sand to blot the ink. Tessa applied all her attention to deciphering the letter, which was a task of considerable difficulty, for the writing was so erratic and the crossing so confused that it was simply impossible to make out every word. She did understand the spirit of the letter, though, and this alarmed her quite enough.

As soon as she was done, she went directly to find her father, finally bringing him to earth in a corner of the impressive two-story library, where he was playing backgammon with Colin.

"I have had a letter from Lady Margaret," she said, coming to the point at once, "and I should like to return to town with you, Papa, for I think that she and her family are in need of a friend."

Sir Edwin's brows knitted. "You know I should be glad to have you with me, Tess, but you must consult with your mother on the matter. What has happened now? I thought that business of Lady Hartfield would have been old news to the gossips by now."

"It would be," Tessa answered grimly, "if the Duke of Gillane were not determined to ruin Lord Hartfield. Meg writes that now there is talk of something more sinister than suicide, and you can guess where the blame is placed and what is the source of the rumors. She also mentioned a visit from Bow Street and the fear that Gillane will use his power to do even worse than try to make Hartfield an outcast."

Colin gave a low whistle. "If it's Bow Street, it must be talk of murder. That is outside of enough!"

Sir Edwin appeared thoughtful. "There is no denying Gillane's very real power in the city and government, but though Bow Street is not incorruptible, it is generally a strict rule that more is needed for them to pursue an inquiry than the vituperation of one embittered man, however rich or wellborn he might be. It must be this way, you know, or we would none of us be safe from our enemies."

"Papa!" cried Tessa, amazed. "Do *you* suppose that Hartfield would murder his wife?"

"If I know anything of character, no," Sir Edwin responded without hesitation. "I didn't say I thought Hartfield guilty, I only believe that Gillane has found some means of making the authorities believe at least that there is probable cause to suspect Hartfield."

"Damn the man!" Tessa said forcefully, not caring what the gentlemen might think of her unladylike exclamation. "*I* don't know whether Hartfield drove Constance to suicide, or put the laudanum in her hand and told her it was hartshorn, but one would think that Gillane would at least have a care for his daughter's reputation. The more this becomes a full-blown public scandal, the more her own less-than-honorable behavior must come to light. I think everyone has suffered enough because of Constance Hartfield."

"Trouble alive, trouble dead," Colin said, succinctly summing up the character of Constance Hartfield. "Gillane's not thinking straight, of course. It's being said in town that he's become touched in his upper works on the subject of Hartfield. Frankly, I shouldn't have thought it of Hartfield. I daresay there may have been times when he'd have liked to throttle that wife of his with great good will. But he don't want for sense that I've ever noticed, and if he'd put up with her that long, I don't see what he'd have to gain by doing her in. Seems to me, in fact, that he's lost a great deal."

Listening to her cousin, Tessa schooled her features to remain motionless. She could well think of a reason why Jonathan Hartfield might suddenly take it into his head to rid himself of his unwanted wife. It was a simpler and in many ways less painful course than divorce, and he could not have known that the duke would take it into his head to hound him to justice. Such thoughts, Tessa told herself firmly, were a betrayal of Margaret and her family, and she pushed them to the back of her mind, where they hovered unheeded even if they did not dissipate.

"I think you are right, Tess, that Hartfield will need friends if the matter has come to this," Sir Edwin said. "If I have learned nothing else from my twenty years at the bar, it is that good evidence is better than guilt to hang a man. Neither Hartfield nor his friends can take for granted that innocence will protect him."

Tess shivered involuntarily and looked up to find Colin staring at her speculatively. Turning to her father, she asked, "Could you help him, Papa?"

"I would be pleased to offer him advice as a friend if he were to come to me, but it would be most unethical for me to offer him assistance in a professional capacity." Seeing Tessa's crestfallen look, he added, "What he truly needs at this moment is a solicitor. I am a barrister, my love, and you know that by the time he would need me, things would have come to a pretty pass indeed."

"I know, Papa," she replied, "and that is exactly what I fear; the duke's determination in this is frightening. But however unofficially, I wish that we might all stand by Lord Hartfield and his family. That is why I feel I must go to town with you. I should be wretched in Pembrokeshire, itching for news and letting my imagination have rein."

Sir Edwin smiled indulgently at his favorite daughter. "Well, love, I shall have a word with your mother, and if you like, you may slip the hint to Meg Caster that Hartfield may come to me if he feels in the need of a confidant."

Tessa impulsively jumped up from the chair on which she had been perched to hug her father. Though Sir Edwin usually gave his wife a free hand with their daughters, when he did interfere with her plans for them, he had his way. Without a doubt of the outcome of this promised exchange, Tessa went up to her bedchamber to see to her packing.

* * *

The morning after her return to London with her father, Tessa called on Lady Margaret and was forced to rudely insist on sending up her card at the least, for the servants had been told most strictly that the family was to be denied to all callers. Margaret herself came downstairs to greet her friend and apologize that instructions had not been left for her exception. "But I did not look to see you until the beginning of March at the earliest," Margaret said as she led her friend upstairs to her own sitting room, one of the few chambers with a fire now that economies had to be practiced.

Almost as soon as the door closed behind them, Margaret's smile of welcome turned to a valiant effort to hold back her tears. Tessa embraced her and allowed her to weep, and when she was ready, pour out her grief and tears, offering what comfort it was in her power to give and feeling dreadfully inadequate.

At about the same time that Lady Margaret was sobbing out her troubles to Tessa, her father was entering Brooks's and heading for the reading room for a quiet hour to read an interesting brief that had come to his chambers that morning.

Edwin Alan Meereswith Bellamy at eight-and-forty was regarded by his peers and the public in general as the premier barrister in the country. Certainly through family connexions if not sheer ability he might by now have been King's Counsel or even risen to the bench, but he had no ambition or desire for either. His fortune was not earned but respectably inherited, though the yeoman stock from which his family had sprung was only three generations in the family's past. His grandfather had been the Bishop of Exeter, his father a Gentleman in the King's own household. He had married the youngest daughter of the then Earl of Dexter and her family had considered the match to be brilliant.

Generally it was frowned upon for any man with pretensions to gentility to have what might be termed a "profession," unless it was the two catch-alls for younger sons, the church and the army. But unlike the profession of solicitor, which, though it did cull younger sons from the aristocracy into its ranks, was seldom treated with the respect the learning of its members should have commanded, that of barrister, whose members were advocates of the law, was held by most laymen with something like awe. They were the elite practitioners of the law and the necessity of special learning and specialized skills to attain success made the profession unexceptionable to even the highest of sticklers.

Sir Edwin's strongly held beliefs and unquestioned integrity had given him the respect and admiration of all his fellows, and most solicitors with clients in need of an advocate courted him shamelessly to persuade him to accept their briefs. Unlike many barristers, Sir Edwin had the luxury to pick and choose the most interesting and the leisure to peruse them in the comfort of his club.

It was still early enough in the day for the company to be thin and the usual buzz of conversation and hum of activity from other parts of the club scarcely penetrated. It happened, then, that the crashing noise, when it came, was all the more startling.

A sleeping man in a nearby chair snorted to life and then buried himself further into the chair to resume his rest; another occupant of the room lowered his book and with a pained expression quitted the room. Sir Edwin, the only other man in the room, glanced up from his brief, and stared for a moment at the doorway from which the sound had come. When it was not repeated and no one seemed inclined to hurry in that direction, he assumed it had been nothing more than a footman involved in a *contretemps* with an overladen tray, and put the matter out of his mind.

But a few minutes later the silence was again shattered, this time by the sound of a man's voice damning in forceful and obscene language some unfortunate other. The reply, if any, was inaudible, but Sir Edwin had recognized the loud voice and knew that its owner was gaining a considerable reputation for the distressing scenes he was creating over the most piddling of causes. Sir Edwin sighed and put aside his brief; given the obvious violence of the Duke of Gillane, he could reasonably guess at the identity of his victim. He rose and went into the hall, following the duke's voice to the room where he might be found. As he neared the door, the second voice became distinct, and even in piecemeal form he was able to perceive the contents of the conversation. Sir Edwin made a grimace of distaste. A footman came into the hall at a trot, but Sir Edwin waved him away and himself entered the room without announcing his presence.

"It is only a matter of time before you are taken up and made to pay," the duke said in a passionate hiss. "You damned viperous leech, I'll . . ." He broke off abruptly as he caught sight of Sir Edwin. "What the devil do you want here?" he demanded imperiously.

"Peace and quiet, principally," Sir Edwin replied in a firm voice that proved him in no way abashed. "Perhaps you are unaware that your voice is carrying considerably beyond this room and is creating a disturbance. Your quarrel with Hartfield," he added with a nod toward Jonathan, who stood silent and grim near the hearth, "is not the concern of this company, and I would not suppose you would care to make it so."

The duke's jaw dropped in visible astonishment. With his wealth and his rank to give him importance and power, it was the rare man who would dare to gainsay him. Sir Edwin, though, stood before him regarding him without any personal concern. He was financially and socially secure enough to place no particular value on the duke's good opinion, and he had fortune and power of his own to counter any vindictiveness the duke might attempt to sit upon him for his impertinence. He did not flinch when the fierce aspect of the duke, a tall man with wiry hair and brows, was turned upon him.

"The devil you say," Gillane said, and it was a low growl. "I know you, don't I? Bellamy, isn't it? Took supper with you at the Clarendon a few months back, wasn't it? Don't let it go to your head, man. I've no argument with you and I've other things to occupy me, so don't presume, and I shan't regard this."

Another man might have flushed at this deliberately nasty snub, but Sir Edwin was made of harder stuff. "Nor have I an argument with you, my lord duke," he said with no sign that he was yet chastened. "However, I have no intention of sitting idly by to listen to abuse hurled at a young man who I have at times regarded in the light of a son. No gentleman would do so."

Hartfield had said nothing at this point. His features had a sucked-in, withdrawn quality that made him look hollow-cheeked and spectral, but at these words a faint smile relieved the severity of his expression. "A champion, sir? I must thank you, but it is both unnecessary and unwise. Gillane hears no promptings beyond those of his personal devil, and I have found the best way to deal with him is to allow his passion to consume itself. Certainly reason does not answer any more than a return of heat."

To the surprise even of Sir Edwin, the duke actually spat on the fine Aubusson carpet. "Damned club isn't fit for gentlemen any longer," he said with great contempt. "It's given over to cits and commoners, cowards and thieves." Though his bile was directed at both of them, Sir Edwin saw the marquis' hands grip the mantel until the knuckles were white, and he put a gentle, steadying hand on his shoulder.

Giving the duke back his own would not answer and would give the gossips even more grist for their mills.

Gillane glowered at each man in turn and then strode from the room, muttering threats and obscenities beneath his breath.

Hartfield visibly relaxed, drooping his shoulders for a moment like a man inexpressibly weary. He stepped over the shards of broken crockery which lay about the hearth and took Sir Edwin's hand. "I do thank you, sir, for your intervention; I know it was kindly meant, but you may regret this day's work. Gillane is determined to see me friendless, and he won't forget that you came to my assistance. He is not a man lightly crossed."

"Neither am I," Sir Edwin said in his dry way. "I fancy I may befriend whom I choose, and I would not care to stand by and watch what I saw today even if you were not the son of a man I held as a dear friend. Take some brandy with me, Hartfield. I know it is early, but then, it is early to be put through the mill as well, and you frankly look as if you could use it."

The corners of Jonathan's mouth lifted slightly and he nodded. He *did* need a friend and was not about to whistle one of this caliber down the rainspout.

Since he had given up his life in town, those of his cronies who had tried to keep up his friendship had found their efforts kindly and politely snubbed and one by one had fallen away. He was a private man, particularly given to introspection when troubled, and he abhorred being an object of pity to others. But only the strictest of hermits do not feel the need to unburden themselves and take the comfort offered by a fellow creature. He followed Sir Edwin to a room farther down the hall.

After Sir Edwin had instructed a hovering, curious

servant to bring them the brandy, the two men made themselves comfortable in chairs near the hearth.

"I have only been returned to town for a day, but I have heard enough of you and Gillane to give me serious concern," the older man said without preamble. "I also understand, from a letter my girl received from Lady Margaret, that there have been men from Bow Street to interview you and a number of the servants."

"And nearly anyone else they could find who might have called himself my friend on the day in question," Jonathan said caustically. "There are few, though, who will now even admit to acquaintance. My mother thinks I am a fool to go about in the world, leaving myself open to cuts and snubs. There are moments when I wonder if she isn't in the right of it."

The servant, his ears flapping, came in with the brandy and glasses and was clearly disappointed at the want of conversation between the two men. Sir Edwin instructed him to close the door behind him, and to be certain that he did, followed him, advising him against hovering in the hall.

"I suppose that was necessary," Jonathan said with a resigned sigh. "I begin to think even the sweeps exchange tidbits about my life. If Gillane has his way, this will be nothing to my future trials."

"Gillane will not have his way unless there is evidence against you. Is there anything which might suggest that you played an active part in the death of your wife?" Sir Edwin asked baldly.

"As far as I know, it is only the word of her dresser, who was also her nursery maid," Jonathan said scornfully. "Not enough to have a poacher taken up without the weight of a man such as Gillane behind it."

"This woman has given testimony against you?" asked Sir Edwin, his tone becoming increasingly businesslike. "Do you know what she has said?"

Jonathan nodded. "Gillane made me a present of it. She claims that the laudanum bottle that was found beside Constance's bed was from a special supply that she had put aside to dole out to her mistress when she had trouble sleeping. To avoid accidents, she insists, should Constance's 'fine sensibilities' become disordered. What she meant, of course, was that she could not trust Connie not to overdose herself when she came home with too much wine." He paused, let out his breath in a short sigh, and then continued. "That may well be the truth, I couldn't say, but the rest is a lie. She has said that she told me of this, and only me, so that I might be able to administer to Connie in . . . more intimate situations. That, of course, is absurd. Connie and I have seldom even lived under the same roof for the past two years; there was no intimacy of any sort between us. But it is her word against mine, and the truth I must face is that at this moment the word of a servant, even one who must be biased against me, would undoubtedly be given credit over mine."

"I wouldn't be certain of that," Sir Edwin said. "That isn't a great deal to make an accusation of murder on. The dresser might have given her the bottle herself and now be afraid to admit it, or for that matter, Lady Hartfield might have discovered it for herself. I shouldn't have my neck measured for a noose on that information. I find it hard even to believe that Gillane was able to persuade Bow Street to act on anything so flimsy."

Jonathan was staring into the glass he held in his hand, but his eyes flicked up to the barrister's at this. "There *is* more. This woman, the duke, my own valet, who has chosen to cast his lot with Gillane— all heard me threaten my wife, and on more than one occasion, that last week of her life. The whole of the household knows that we fought incessantly when I was there at all, and that Constance, for her part, threatened to ruin me repeatedly. She told her woman that she believed that it was my wish to kill her."

Sir Edwin tilted his head with curiosity. "You surprise me, Hartfield. I would not have guessed at such behavior in you, from what I know of your character. Not that you are incapable of becoming impassioned, but—"

"You thought me a cold fish," Jonathan said before he could finish.

"I would have said that you have self-command."

Jonathan shrugged. "It is much the same thing." He sipped at the brandy. "The histrionics were Connie's. Only once or twice did she break my temper, and that was only briefly. When I told her I meant to rid myself of her, I meant divorce, not murder. She understood that, and she said to me, too, time and again, that if she were held up publicly for her infidelities, she would as soon I murdered her. She could not comprehend that this time she had no power over me, that I didn't give a damn for the opinion of the world or the comforts her fortune could buy. Divorce, not her death, is what I wished for."

"Why?"

Jonathan's lids came down over his eyes in a way that Tessa would have recognized at once. "If you know anything of my history, you must know the answer to that."

"I know that you found yourself in a situation that could not have been comfortable, but was hardly uncommon," Sir Edwin replied blandly. "If Lady Hartfield was unfaithful to you, she was no less discreet than most, and if there was a bit more talk this last time than before, it still was not open scandal. Why should you suddenly wish for divorce, when the two of you seemed to have worked out your differences in separation? Is there someone else?"

"No," Jonathan said shortly. He might now have confided to Sir Edwin the reasons he had had for putting his wife aside, but the words would not come to his tongue. He never doubted that he might trust Sir Edwin completely with this secret, and at least it was obvious to him that Tessa had held her peace as she had said she would. But partly from his own pride and partly because now that Constance was dead he saw no point in making her disgrace known to anyone, he diverged from the truth. "It is common belief that I married my wife for her money, and in truth, I could not have wed her if she had had no portion, but if I am a cold fish, it is because of the experience of the mess that giving sway to my passions has brought me. If it was anything that made me decide to end my marriage, it was my pride and feelings of self-worth, or perhaps the want of this. I knew that the exchange of my comfort for my complaisance was no longer to me a fair bargain. There was, as you say, more talk with Sir Richard and less discretion as well. I decided it was enough."

Sir Edwin put his glass on a table by his chair, and regarded the younger man in silence for a few moments. "I can't say where this thing will go for you, Hartfield, but that it could even have come this far tells me that it is not to be taken lightly. I think you would be wise to consult your solicitor."

"The man who acted for me is Gillane's man."

"Then if you wish it, I shall recommend a few good men to you," the barrister offered. "But more to the moment, I think it might be best if you were to go to a friend for a time, preferably one that it would not be obvious for you to seek out."

Jonathan's eyes narrowed still further. "Are you suggesting that arrest might be imminent and that I deliberately hide out to avoid it?" he asked plainly.

"What I am suggesting is as a friend rather than a barrister," Sir Edwin replied, "but as a barrister I can say I do not care for this situation. If Bow Street is in on it, then it is only because Gillane is pushing it, and if he has gone this far, I don't believe he will rest until he has you brought up on charges. If you have told me everything you know he has against you, it is flimsy enough evidence, but enough, I think, at least to see you in Newgate, if not enough to convict you." He saw Jonathan blanch slightly and added quickly, "That is why it is best for you to leave the city for a time, or at least go to a place where you will not be found out. I cannot help you professionally until there are charges against you and a brief made up, but as a friend I will do whatever is in my power to assist your attorney to have this nonsense quashed as it should be. I can see you do not care for the idea, but I think you would like making yourself scarce better than being in a common cell in Newgate. Gillane can pay to see to it that you get no comforts there if he chooses, and though that may be countered, it could give you a few exceptionally unpleasant days at first. Take my advice in this, Hartfield. I assure you it is sound."

"I don't doubt it, sir," Jonathan answered, and added with a self-mocking smile, "In fact, you quite terrify me, but you see, there is nowhere I may go. I have little family beyond my sister and mother, and what friends remain to me would not, I think, extend their regard for me to the length of breaking the law themselves by harbouring me."

"It would hardly be a question of harbouring until there was a formal issue for your arrest," said Sir Edwin, "but in any case, if friends and family won't answer, I could lend you a sum to take you out of the country for a time. It could be arranged."

"That I will not do," Jonathan said positively. "Playing least in sight is one thing, running away quite another."

Sir Edwin saw by the mulish expression on the other's face that pursuing this course would be pointless. He sighed and tapped a thoughtful forefinger against the side of his nose. "Why don't you have a bit more of the brandy, Hartfield? It won't hurt a strong young head like yours. I need to think on this a bit."

"I thank you, sir," Jonathan said respectfully, "but it is not necessary for you to tax yourself in this matter. Your advice has already been invaluable to me and I am in your debt for your concern."

"If you feel I am offering you a sort of charity," Sir Edwin said shrewdly, "you are mistaken. What I do is for your father as much as for you, and because men like Gillane, who imagine that power has no purpose but to satisfy their own whims, cannot be allowed to destroy others with less resources."

Sir Edwin then fell into a silence which Jonathan did not presume to break. He remained very quiet, sipping his brandy and pursuing his own thoughts while the lawyer applied his considerable talents to the difficulties at hand.

Chapter Four

Tessa awoke from a light sleep and listened carefully for the thumping noise that had awakened her to occur again. It did not, but she thought she heard a different sort of sound, and curiously, it seemed to come from the other side of the wall behind her bed. Still disoriented from sleep, she placed no significance on this for a moment or so until she was more wakeful and realized that the only thing that should have been on the other side of the wall was an empty room. In fact it was the dressing room that had been hers when she had occupied the bedchamber connecting to it.

There were not, as far as she knew, any guests in the house. More curious than alarmed, she got out of bed, and donning her slippers and a silk wrapper, she went out into the dark hall. No light shone from under the door and she cautiously tried the handle but found the door locked. This did puzzle her, and she moved farther down the hall to the door of the connecting bedchamber. This opened readily enough, and moving silently through the room, she tried the other door to the dressing room and discovered that locked as well.

She simply stood there for a few minutes pondering this oddity and wondering if there might be something to give her concern, and if there were, what she should do about it. After a few moments, though, one solution to the mystery occurred to her. It was not uncommon for illicit romance to spring up between members of the staff, nor for them to fix up trysting places in unused corners of the house to avoid detection.

Sighing, Tessa returned to the corridor. Unpleasant as it might be, the situation would have to be dealt with, and at once. Lady Frances was a stickler for correct conduct among her staff, and if this were to come to her ears, which was inevitable, given time, both would be turned out without a character. Pursing her lips at the distasteful chore ahead of her, she quietly returned to her room.

She found her tinderbox and relit her bed candle. Carrying this over to her dressing table, she drew out her jewel box and rummaged through it until she found a small ring of keys. She selected one of them, blew out the candle, and padded out into the hall again to the other room.

Pausing a moment to collect her thoughts for what she would say and her emotions for what she might find, she inserted the key quietly into the lock of the dressing-room door. Gingerly she turned the handle and pushed against the door.

As the door cracked, light spilled out of the room, but the door did not open easily, as if something impeded it, an object, Tessa thought, to keep the light from showing beneath the door. Without warning, the door was pulled from her grasp and swung swiftly inward.

The light in the room was not bright, but it was a sharp contrast to the darkness she had been in a moment ago and she bowed her head from it to give her eyes a moment to adjust. But the room, she saw in one brief glance, had indeed been made into a makeshift bedchamber, and she thought her suspicions confirmed. She raised her head again, expecting to find the guilty couple before her, but the sight that did greet her took her breath away in one sharp gasp. Her hand clutched to her heart in fine dramatic tradition, and Jonathan Hartfield broke into a reluctant smile.

"My mamma could not have responded in finer style," he told her, and because she understood him even in her amazement, she could not help but return his smile.

"But *I* shall not now succumb to the vapours," she replied. "Or at least I don't think I shall; it will depend on your reason for being here, I think, for even a *gentleman* thief would be an unsavory thing to encounter."

"Is that what you think? That I am here to nab the silver? I have chosen an odd place to look for it, I think, and in any case, though I am far from stout in the pocket, I haven't come to *that* yet."

"Jewels, then," Tessa suggested, but added, "I don't think it, but it is the only thing I could think of, however farfetched, unless . . ." She stopped and pondered her thought, looking at him speculatively.

"Unless?" he prompted.

"I think it might be best if you simply told me what you *are* doing here," she said coolly. "There is, of course, a reason."

"Of course!" he agreed amiably. "What an admirable young woman you are, Miss Bellamy, no vapours and a calm demand of my motives. Almost you give me hope."

He turned his back and went farther into the room. Tessa followed him. "Of what?" she asked curiously.

He had been thinking of the manner in which his mother, wife, or even his sister would have reacted in a similar situation and what would have been his awkward position if Tessa had behaved in any similar way. It had boosted his opinion of her and of her sex. "Would you care for wine, Miss Bellamy?" he asked over his shoulder as he stood in front of a small desk which held a decanter and two glasses. "It may seem odd in me to be offering you refreshment in your home and in such circumstances, but then, everything about this situation is odd, don't you agree?"

His flip manner made her suspect for a moment that he was castaway, but his eyes when he turned to look at her were quite clear, and there was no other indication that he was jug-bitten. She nodded agreement to the wine and said, "That is stating the obvious. Do you wish me to close the door? I don't believe anyone is up and about now, but I left the door into the bedchamber open, and some trace of this light might penetrate to the hall."

He handed her a glass and indicated two wing chairs pushed into a corner of the small room. "Are you so sure my presence here is innocent that you care to be that alone with me?" he asked quizzingly.

"It is obvious to me that you are here at the invitation of someone," Tessa said, sitting. "The room had been made into a bedchamber for you with as much comfort as possible. You have wine in one of our own crystal decanters and two glasses; two chairs that I never knew to be in this room before have been put here so that you might be comfortable with a visitor. It is impossible that you could have expected me; for Mamma or Letty to know of your presence is equally absurd. It must be Papa, and therefore there is a very sensible reason for this, for Papa never does things in a catch-as-catch-can manner."

A slow smile spread over his features and even touched his curiously colored eyes. "Perspicacious as well." He raised his glass. "I salute you, Miss Bellamy."

Her eyes narrowed suspiciously. "Are you mocking me, my lord?"

"No, Miss Bellamy, I am admiring you," he replied with alacrity. "But I would prefer it if you would address me by my given name and allow me to call you Tess. It compounds the absurdity of this intimate meeting to address each other with such formality."

"If you wish," she said, and brushed this aside for more important matters. "It is Papa who has brought you here, is it not? Why?"

"Because he felt this was a more comfortable prison than Newgate."

Tessa's lips parted in surprise. "What do you mean?"

"Oh, come, Tess, don't disappoint me now," he admonished. "If you think on it for a moment, I know you will come to the answer without my assistance."

He regarded her from over the rim of his glass, his eyes challenging her, and Tessa took up the gauntlet. After a few minutes' cogitation she began to tentatively speak her conclusions. "You are going to be taken in charge for the murder of Constance." She paused and met his eyes, her own wide. "Dear Lord! I cannot believe it!"

"Believe it," he advised caustically. "Go on."

"Papa believes you innocent, and has decided to help you keep from prison," she said, "but that is as much as I understand. He cannot suppose that such a serious charge will be forgotten in your absence, and it would be impossible for you to stay here indefinitely."

"I should hope it would," he said with some feeling. "It is not that I do not appreciate the hospitality, or would find Newgate more diverting, but hanging might have some appeal after living a lonely upside-down life in one room for any length of time." He finished off the wine in his glass and placed the empty glass on the desk, which he could reach by stretching out his arm. "What is it to be, then? Do you approve of your father's sudden departure from upholding the law? Will you run from me and raise the alarm to have me cast into the street?"

Tessa was not entirely sure what she thought of this, but she knew she was not frightened and did not object. As she sat across from him and watched him speak, she saw the flickering candlelight putting warmth into his usually cool eyes and adding depths of burnished gold to his hair, and was aware more than ever what an exceptionally attractive man he was. This did alarm her, and though it was not enough to make her leave him, it was enough to put a businesslike briskness in her tone. "If it is what Papa wishes, I shall not question him."

"You are a most obedient daughter," he commented. "But if you found me out so easy, and even possess a key to this apartment, then I think it is likely I shall be found out again even with your silence."

"I shouldn't think so," Tessa said, and then explained to him about the noises she had heard, why she would have a key to the room, and what had led her to investigate.

He smiled at the last part of her story but then turned suddenly serious. "I know you have spoken with my sister, and I don't doubt you have heard the gossip. Do you think I murdered my wife, Tess?"

Tessa was a bit taken aback both by the sudden change in his manner and by the turn of the conversation. She was startled into saying exactly what she thought. "I have no idea."

"But surely you have an opinion."

Tessa did not answer him. Instead she asked what had occurred to cause her father to bring him to their house in this surreptitious way. He told her the complete truth without hesitation, and when he was done, Tessa did not comment but asked, "You did not tell Papa about the child?"

"No."

"Why not?"

He got up to fetch more wine for them both. "I don't want that brought into this at all if possible. It is a disgrace for Constance and an added scandal to me. If Constance did die by her own hand, then it may be pertinent to her motive, but it can't be anything but harmful to me, for if it were known, it would most certainly be pertinent to *my* motive."

Tessa agreed that this was so, and when Jonathan then asked if she meant to keep his secret, she replied that she would, and added, "Though I do think you might tell Papa, for he always says that a barrister can only truly help his client when he knows all the truth."

"Not, I think, when the truth favors guilt," he said dryly. "It may be moot in any case, for there is Sir Richard to consider; but it is my understanding that he is hiding out too, in Ireland, intending to distance himself and his name as far from this mess as a few hundred miles can take him." He sat down again and said, "But you have not answered my question. What is your opinion of my guilt or innocence?"

This time Tessa considered for a moment before replying. "Well, at the least, I am certain that there must have been times when you would wish to murder her," she said in her straightforward way. "I might believe you had finally done so if she had been shot or stabbed in a passion, but cold-blooded, premeditated murder? It is not impossible, I think, but also not likely."

"In short, you can imagine me killing in the heat of the moment," he said with surprise, "but not with calculation. How strange! One of Connie's most consistent complaints against me was that she found me too cold."

"I think rather that you are controlled," Tessa said, unconsciously echoing the opinion of her parent. "But if you did do it in that way," she went on meditatively, "I would think that you did it in the same spirit that you married her. Knowing what was necessary and acting boldly, trusting that you would carry the thing off.''

This speech was an impertinence that amounted to insolence, and it was the easy intimacy of their discussion that had made her tongue so unguarded. As soon as the words were spoken, she regretted them, for as at the last time when she had unintentionally given him offense, at Letitia's ball, his expression changed abruptly. "I beg your pardon," she said sincerely, for it mattered to her that their easy camaraderie not evaporate. "I should not have said such a thing."

"No, you should not," he said crisply. "I cannot help what the world assumes of my marriage, but I expect it to have the breeding to keep its opinion to itself."

The words were stinging, and meant to be so, but Tessa knew they were deserved. She gave a small shaky laugh. "You really should not mind your image as wicked fortune hunter. It is quite romantic, you know, dashing and dangerous, and devastatingly attractive." Again she nearly bit her wayward tongue as this time her chagrin betrayed her. It did not require a powerful degree of perception to read the speculation that was in his expression now.

"Then you are most intrepid," Jonathan said levelly and softly. "It was my understanding that fortune hunters were held up as monsters to be avoided at all costs, but if for you the image has allure, then this is bearding the ogre in his den indeed."

"I think it has allure for most heiresses," she said as calmly as she could. "The lure of forbidden fruit, you see. But if I have weathered three seasons without running off with a half-pay officer—the most dangerous and enticing of all—then I think I may safely trust myself with you."

He laughed softly. "Do not underestimate the lure

of an impoverished marquis. We make up in rank what we concede to dash.''

His light treatment of her words brought them back to an easy footing, and her impertinence and her unintentional admission of her attraction to him were allowed to be forgotten.

This conversation was only the first of many between them in the next fortnight. Impelled by the lure of that attraction and by a genuine pleasure in his company, she visited him nightly, careful that the rest of the household, and in particular Ardly, her father's valet, who was nobly keeping odd hours himself to attend the marquis, had at last retired for the night.

There was a tacit understanding between them that neither would mention these visits to her father, who, under the impression that his clandestine guest must be bored to flinders with no company but his own, snatched what time he could to spend with the young man. The more he came to know Jonathan, the more he felt his opinion of him confirmed, but fond father though he was, he would not at all have understood these midnight visits and might have placed on them a complexion that did not at all exist.

Or perhaps it was on the surface that it did not exist. Jonathan was the sort of person who gave his thoughts away as gifts. Tessa, who tried not to lie to herself, admitted that the attraction was more than friendship, but if her feelings were reciprocated, she had no evidence. There were times when he would look at her in that speculative way of the first night and at times he would openly flirt with her, but whether this was diversion or regard, she could never be certain.

She was very much aware of the danger of these visits, both emotionally and physically. The more time she spent with him, the more she wished to be with him; when they were not together, he was in her thoughts. She stored up the happenings of her

day as tidbits to share with him, and found that
days turned upside down so that she could be with
him in the night were no hardship. In fact, her
looking glass told her she suffered not at all from
snatched rest instead of regular sleep.

Tessa did not quite say to herself: You are falling
in love with him. But she knew the truth of the
matter and in this lay the danger. She had never
wanted for suitors, and a few of these had succeeded in maneuvering her into lonely corners to
impress upon her their impassioned speeches and
feverish kisses, and a few of these had not been
entirely unwelcome, but for the first time in her life
she knew she wanted something more from a man
than his friendship. She did not give her feelings a
name, but she understood them and knew that should
he wish for more than friendship between them, she
would offer him no resistance. She did not actually
think of marriage, for that was for the future, and
his future was too untenable, but she hadn't a doubt
that she had at last found the man with whom she
could happily spend the remainder of her life.

Two things made this surreptitious activity possible.
Her mother and Letitia were still in Pembrokeshire
and the want of company in town made her staying
in of evenings seem perfectly normal. There was the
occasional dinner or assembly that she might have
attended, and in fact, Colin, who had returned to
town shortly after Tessa and her father, tried on a
few occasions to persuade her that she should be out
more, but she was content as she was.

Yet every idyll must have an imperfection, and in
this one it came when Jonathan had been in the
Bellamy house just over a fortnight. His humor on
one night was quiet and rather moody. She supposed that this must be inevitable in his situation,
but it continued for the next two nights and his
manner became increasingly sarcastic and even bitter.

After the first night they had begun the practice of

not mentioning his reason for being in the house or the difficulties of his past or the uncertainties of his future. Their conversation was always light and bantering, weighty only on impersonal issues. She did not doubt that it was his problems that were making him so dispirited, and supposed that the news her father brought him of his efforts on his behalf must be discouraging.

Since she felt constrained from discussing the matter with Jonathan, she went instead to her father, treading warily, for she knew how perceptive Sir Edwin could be and feared giving herself away. Fortunately, she was successful in not awakening his suspicions; unfortunately, she heard from her father what she had feared she might and had hoped she would not.

Despite the considerable efforts of Mr. Ryder, the solicitor who as a good friend of Sir Edwin had taken on Jonathan with enthusiasm and dedication, the charges were not to be dropped against him. The duke was throwing about his weight to its full extent in his determination to punish his son-in-law, and it was becoming obvious that there was nothing that would successfully hinder him.

"He is a powerful man, Tess," Sir Edwin reiterated, "and he is not only using that power but the whole of his fortune. I can't know what this is costing him pound and pence, but I'll wager it was more than Hartfield ever cost him in all the time he was married to his daughter."

For the first time the hollowness of fear clutched at Tessa. "Then what is to happen, Papa?" she asked, unable to wholly keep the tremor out of her voice. "Will Lord Hartfield hang?"

"I shouldn't think so," said Sir Edwin, unaware that his failure to utter a firm negative had given his daughter grief. "But I shall not assume success against the flimsiness of the evidence as I did at first. Nothing would have come of this, I am sure, without

Gillane to push it. Having gotten his way this far, he won't stop at trying for the conviction as well."

"I know the Casters are saying that Lord Hartfield is staying with friends, but the duke is putting it about that he has run away rather than face up to the accusation he has made against him," Tessa said carefully, deliberately treading on dangerous ground. "Is it true, Papa, is it desperate enough that he should run away?"

Sir Edwin shook his head and smiled, no more giving away that he knew of the marquis' whereabouts than had his daughter. "He would be foolish indeed to run away. He would spend the rest of his life a nameless fugitive, and as likely as not, for nothing. There *is* risk that in facing up to the charges he will be convicted. There must always be that risk, but in this case I believe it small enough to chance. Since he is a peer, he will not be tried in a court of law, but before the Lords, and Gillane cannot buy or coerce enough of them to have his way. Already his excesses are leaving a bad taste in people's mouths. At the moment, opinion is against Hartfield, but I shall be very surprised if that does not change by the time this mess is done."

While her father's words were not precisely discouraging, neither did Tessa find them particularly encouraging. Nor was she at all surprised at the lowering mood that had of late been upon Jonathan; he had agreed to Sir Edwin's scheme to put himself out of the way in the hope that the matter might be resolved without his incarceration or a trial. Now those hopes were dashed, and worse, he was being branded a coward for his absence.

The interview with her father had taken place in the morning, and the evening was taken up with a card party at the Cowpers', which Colin had badgered her into attending, but the portion of the day in between seemed to her nearly interminable. Even the party and variety of company did not truly divert her and she surprised and annoyed her cousin by insisting that they leave early. But once she was home, she wished that she had listened to Colin, for Sir Edward was quite late returning home that evening and she did not dare go to Jonathan until she could feel certain that her father was in his bed for the night. She sat in her darkened room, listening for the sounds of her father's return, and mused on what she would say to Jonathan about the information she had gleaned that afternoon.

Jonathan, too, sat in a room lighted only by what feeble light a half-moon could cast through the panes of the room's single window. He stared at the dark, blank wall of his mother's house with a matching blankness in his expression. The hopes with which he had entered this house were entirely dissipated and the only solace he could find was in a bottle, though such a thing was not his usual way of dealing with defeat. In the normal way he believed in cutting his losses and going on, but the problem was that this time there could be no guarantee that there was a future for him to go on to. It was hard to gird oneself for an ordeal knowing that there might be nothing to grasp on to when it was past.

He was not yet castaway, but he meant to be. In part his behavior was self-punishment. In the past fortnight, he had allowed himself to have hopes about more than just his own freedom from the burden his wife's death and her father's vindictiveness had placed upon him. Now, in his depression of spirits, he castigated himself as a fool not only for his dreams but also because they were of the sort that made him fear he did not learn from his mistakes.

When he at last heard Tessa's tapping at his door, he ignored it. Tessa, fearing that he had been spirited out of the house during her absence and that she would not again see him until after he had had his judgment by the House of Lords, again felt icy fingers clutching at her. She did not know what manner of understanding she had hoped to achieve with him this night, but she feared his being gone and the changes this would mean to the relationship that had been developing between them if there was none. She knocked more sharply and insistently, aware that the sound might penetrate to other parts of the house, but not caring.

The door swung open easily, for there was no need for a barrier to keep in the light. "Jonathan?" she said uncertainly, surprised at the total darkness of the room.

He stood in the doorway, not moving aside for her. "It is late and I didn't think to see you tonight," he said with no warmth at all in his tone. "It would be best if you did not stay; I'm not really fit to receive you."

"Are you foxed?" she asked baldly and without censure. "If Papa has told you what he told me this morning, I cannot say I blame you, but it won't do, you know. It is just Dutch comfort and will only add self-loathing to your other problems." She pushed past him and went to the desk to place the stopper in the decanter, which, instead of being nearly full as it usually was on her visits, was now nearly empty.

He did not further protest her presence, nor her presuming to control his behavior. He closed the door and sat in one of the chairs. "Was it wise to discuss me with your father?" he asked, making their shared knowledge—that her visits were most improper—open between them for the first time.

"I was very careful," she assured him. "I had to do so. I could see that you have been upset these last few days and I could guess what it was, but you do not wish to discuss—"

"No, I do not," he interrupted in a tone that bore no patience for argument.

"Then we need not," she said agreeably. Some instinct told her that it *might* be wisest for her to leave him, but she refused to heed it. "I haven't been going out much of late, you know," she said conversationally to begin a neutral and, she hoped, diverting topic, "but my cousin, Colin McAffe, persuaded me that I should enjoy the card party the Cowpers gave this evening. It is still early, but you would be surprised how much company is already in town." She then went on to tell him of the party and the people she had met there, deliberately keeping her tone as light as possible and embellishing situations for his amusement.

She was sitting at the foot of the narrow bed. He sat almost directly across from her, watching her in the darkness as she spoke. She found it a bit disconcerting to be sitting in the dark in this odd way, but she wished to give him no cause to insist on her leaving, so she objected to nothing, not even when he removed the stopper from the decanter again and poured more wine.

He said nothing while she spoke except to answer one or two direct questions, and the thing that gave her the greatest unease was the fact that while she sat in the subdued moonlight, he was in complete shadow and she had no idea what was in his mind while she spoke. He was always a difficult man to read unless he chose to be read, and Tessa didn't doubt that his choice of darkness was quite deliberate.

She had nearly run out of things to say on the subject of the party and was casting about her mind for another safe topic when he at last spoke voluntarily. "Do you often go out escorted by your cousin?" he asked in a voice devoid of inflection, so that she could not tell whether an affirmative answer would be displeasing to him or not.

She decided on honesty. "Yes. Colin and I are very good friends and enjoy each other's company."

"How old are you, Tess? One-and-twenty, I think you told me. You are not only an heiress but a very lovely one . . . you are lively and intelligent. I find it very difficult to believe that you have yet to throw your cap over the windmill."

"I might have if I chose," she admitted, "but I do not dislike my present estate and see no reason to trade it hastily so that the world will not condemn me as an ape leader. I would rather be happy in my choice than quick."

"If you are so fond of McAffe," he said, still speaking softly and levelly, "I would have thought him a tailor-made husband for you."

"I did form a schoolgirl *tendre* for him before my come-out," she said with a light laugh. "He *is* so very handsome, but I think we were meant to be friends to each other, not lovers."

"Yes every good love relationship begins or at least develops in friendship. It would not be an impossible matching, I think," he said ruminatively.

Tessa did not care for this discussion and said rather brusquely, "No," and then, recalling that she did not wish to give him cause to send her from him, she added in a bantering tone, "You know, I have told you I am the darling of half-pay officers. I would not be unfaithful to my admirers by marrying out of their ranks."

"Ah, yes," he said self-mockingly, "I recall that conversation. I informed you that down-at-heel marquises had greater cachet."

"Perhaps, but none has ever made me an offer," she said archly, intentionally quizzing him.

The room was narrow enough for him to be able to reach across it for her hand. "Will you do me the dubious honor of becoming my wife, Miss Bellamy? I promise to shower upon you every comfort your money can buy, and if you give me your pledge to do nothing to disgrace me, I shall give you mine not to dose you with laudanum."

Tessa's heart was beating so hard and fast in her breast that she knew he must feel it in her pulse. She knew that he did not mean his words and was mocking them both, but she felt there was at least a small hint of seriousness in his tone and prayed that it was not just because she wished it so. "What would you do if I said yes?" she queried recklessly.

He laughed mirthlessly in his throat and got up to come sit beside her on the bed. Before she even realized what he was about, Tessa found herself enfolded in his arms and his lips against her own as he kissed her, not awkwardly in a snatched moment as she had known kisses before, but with a gentle intensity that she had never experienced.

His sudden behavior surprised her, and at the same time, it did not. She felt not as if she were swept up in an unexpected wave, but merely cresting on one long swell of passion that had ever been present but simply unacknowledged. The taste, the feel, the warmth of his mouth was heady and completely irresistible.

He released her partially and regarded her, his silvery eyes catching the moonlight in an oddly attractive way. "You should have run away from me that first night, Tess," he said quietly. "Run away from me now before it is too late."

Tessa spoke almost without conscious volition. "I do not wish to run."

"And I have not the will to make you," he said deeply, and once again took her mouth with his.

From that moment, she was past words. At first tentatively, and then with all the desperate, long-suppressed passion his kiss released, she put her arms around him and clung to him. Their mutual caresses were exquisitely tender, yet feverishly impatient as they sought to learn one another's bodies as well as they knew one another's minds. But at last, gently, Jonathan slid her dressing gown and then her nightdress from her shoulders and she was naked to the waist. Her nipples hardened in the cool night air and drew his lips to their nectar. Tendrils of sensations she had not known existed in her before rippled throughout her body, and for the first time in her life she understood what was meant by desire. With lips parted in anticipation, she spoke his name softly and lay back against the pillows, completely and absolutely succumbing to its lure.

Chapter Five

Tessa awoke the next morning feeling like a child on the day of a promised treat. Though it had been in the very small hours of the morning that she had returned to her own bed, she felt completely refreshed and alert.

She believed she had no illusions about what had occurred between her and Jonathan. There had been no words of love exchanged, no promises or commitments. It would be wrong to say that this did not matter to her, for it did, but if she could not say he had had any ennobling reasons for making love to her, she knew that her lovemaking had been the sincere expression of her caring and desire for him.

But her mature and sensible attitude toward their intimacy was not unflawed; like any green girl caught up in the throes of her first love, she could not help heeding the urgings of her heart, which told her that he did care but was in no position to speak. Her head made game of this, trying to crush any foolish illusions she might harbour of a future for them, but her heart was too powerful. If she did not feel secure of him, at least she hoped.

She had half-promised to attend a waltzing party, the after-breakfast entertainment that had become all the crack since that daring dance had gained in popularity, but more than a want of sleep urged her to remain at home, and she dashed off a note of regret.

As the day passed, her impatience to be again with Jonathan grew; by late afternoon she had even convinced herself that whatever he might say to her next, she would know when they met whether it was her head or her heart she might believe. This increased her impatience to the point of anxiety.

As the dinner hour neared, most activity on the upper floors of the Bellamy house ceased, as household chores in that region were finished and it was not yet time for the ritual of dressing for dinner to make up the next round of busywork. Being as cautious as she could, Tessa slipped into the unused bedroom. She knew he slept for most of the daylight hours to minimize the chance of detection and for the convenience of the servant who attended him. She intended to knock quietly, and if he were not awake, or aroused by this, she would be content to wait until her usual time.

She put her knuckles to the panel, and to her amazement, the door swung in a bit. She pushed the door open the rest of the way, and what she beheld was as shocking to her as the night she had first seen this room made up for his comfort. The bed and extra chairs were gone. The writing desk which had served him as a table was folded and against the wall. It was once again an unexceptional apartment awaiting the next occupant of the guest bedchamber.

Tessa could have no idea of the exact moment of his departure, and for some reason this troubled her almost more than the fact that he was gone. She longed to go to her father to ask him if his leaving had been planned or if it had been Jonathan's own decision or perhaps even impulse. He had certainly not so much as hinted to her last night that he would be gone with the morning. But there was no one she could safely ask and nothing she could do but wait and see what information came her way.

Tessa returned to her own room and shortly afterward dressed for dinner. She and her father were dining alone, after which she was to attend an assembly with an aunt and cousin, and she was already dressed to go downstairs when a footman came to announce the arrival of Colin. Tessa was surprised at the hour of his visit, but went to him at once.

She found him waiting for her with evident concern in his expression. "I was almost afraid to find you laid low," he said, taking her hands, "but you look hale enough."

"Of course I am! Why should I not be?"

"You cried off from Betsy Langford's waltz party this morning—she told me when I saw her this afternoon—and you made such a thing of leaving last night that I thought perhaps you were unwell."

"I am afraid it is just whimsy, not illness," Tessa said, touched by his concern. "I do admit, though, that I have not been in spirits of late," she added to explain her behavior. "Perhaps I am missing Letty's chatter."

"Considering what it consisted of when we were at Boxwood, I would have thought her visit to Pembrokeshire would be a blessed relief," he said caustically, for he had found Letitia's condescension toward her sister grating.

"Oh, I don't truly mind Letty's nonsense," Tessa said, laughing. "Do you know that she realized the last day we were at Boxwood that she would now be able to sit above me when dining formally. She said I must not mind this, though, for it is a meaningless convention."

Colin laughed at his younger cousin's absurdities. "The one hope I hold out for the chit is that the scales will drop from Torrance's eyes and he will beat her soundly and regularly," he said with a shocking want of Christian feeling, and at the dark look this brought him, responded, "Yes, I know I should not say so, but it is only to you that I do."

"But you should not," Tessa admonished, and then confided, "I suppose I must confess that I have thought it might be a good thing myself."

"You expect them back soon, don't you?" he asked, and this led to a discussion of family matters that were trivial enough for Tessa to respond to mechanically while her mind engaged other thoughts, principally those of Jonathan.

". . . and then Prinny jumped out of the balloon and floated down to the Hyde Park Pavilion by holding on to his coattails," Colin finished in bland accents.

Tessa, who had caught only the last words of his speech, had a belated feeling that there was something not quite right about what Colin had said. "What did Prinny do to his coattails?" she asked with a small frown of puzzlement. "He isn't trying a new fashion to confound George Brummel again, is he?

Colin sighed. "No, dearest love, but you are certainly confounding me when you go off into a daydream in the middle of our conversation. If you do not find my conversation sparkling and stimulating, you need only say so," He added, sounding mildly injured.

Tessa smiled and begged his pardon, and after a few more minutes Colin rose to leave for a dinner party where he was expected. But as he did so, Lady Margaret was announced and in a moment was with them.

Tessa sighed at the announcement and wondered what her father would think at having his dinner put back by this further interruption, but the moment she set eyes on her friend, all such concern vanished, for it was obvious at once from Margaret's mien that she was in great distress. Colin offered to leave them in privacy, but Margaret insisted that he remain.

It took some minutes for Lady Margaret to state the reason for her visit, and then only with the help of Tessa's prompting, for it was clearly difficult for her to speak on the matter at all. "Jonathan has come back," she said flatly when she did speak. "He simply walked into the house two hours ago, refusing to say where he has been or why he left, and then he sent a message, I don't know to whom, but two men came to the house not an hour past, and they have taken him to Bow Street and from there I fear to Newgate." Her voice broke on the last word and her tears could no longer be held. Colin and Tessa exchanged glances that had very different meanings for each, and the latter applied herself to comforting her friend.

Tessa felt in need of comfort herself, and her eyes pleaded with Colin to remain, even though it was beyond the time for his engagement. He obliged and added his might to easing the fears and anxieties of Lady Margaret.

It was nearly a half-hour before Lady Margaret was able to find her composure, assisted by the arrival in the room of Sir Edwin, who was becoming quite sharpset and concerned that a late dinner would keep him from an engagement he was promised to. He greeted her news with apparent surprise and dismay, but his daughter, carefully watching him, saw that this was show and that he knew perfectly well what had occurred.

It was Sir Edwin's commiseration and professional reassurances that finally gave the distraught young woman some degree of ease. Having unburdened herself and found comfort that she certainly would not receive at home, she did not remain longer and in fact over the protests of the others that it was of no moment, apologized for having disturbed them at so unpropitious a time.

"I suppose that damned woman," Sir Edwin said, speaking his opinion of the dowager plainly, "has been giving the poor girl as much grief in this matter as the arrest itself did. I'll send word to the kitchen that we'll be eating now, shall I?" he added pointedly, and left Tessa and Colin alone again.

Tessa was not the sort of person to seek out a confidant for her troubles when these ran deep. She had no natural one in her immediate family and a habitual reserve made her inclined to rely on her own resources rather than seeking the advice of others. But if time and circumstances had allowed, she might now have unburdened herself to Colin. He was undoubtedly the closest and best loved of her friends and she knew that he would treat her disclosures with loving understanding and no stern judgments.

She had been expecting something of the sort to occur from nearly the moment she had found Jonathan gone, but the reality of it was harder to bear than she had imagined it would be. She stood beside her cousin near the door and realized with a start that a considerable silence had fallen between them. She sought his eyes guiltily, and found there evident concern.

"*Is* something the matter, Tess?" he asked.

"No," she said with a smile, for the momentary desire to bare her feelings had passed. "I am, of course, a bit upset by Meg's news."

"It's a damn shame this thing has come to such a pass," Colin agreed, and added, "Do you think that he killed Constance?"

Tessa's heart sank further that even Colin could ask such a question. "I am sure I have no idea," she said repressively, "and I think his friends at the least must presume him innocent and not indulge in gossip at his expense."

Colin was a bit startled by her attack. "I only asked *you* a question. I do not call that idle gossip. In any case, I shall further expose myself by saying that I could at the least understand it if he had. She must have made him a maddening wife."

"Judge not, lest ye be judged." Tessa reminded him.

"A direct hit," he admitted, laughing, "and the point is taken." He kissed her lightly and left, but his friends, who good-naturedly accepted his apologies when he finally arrived, noted the distraction that remained with him for the rest of the evening.

The weeks that followed were every bit as taxing as Tessa had feared they would be. The principal topic of conversation wherever members of the ton gathered in groups of two or two hundred was the return, arrest, and imminent trial before the House of Lords of Jonathan Hartfield.

The Caster ladies, very naturally, remained in seclusion, but anyone with any connexion to them either by blood or affection was a much-sought-after guest at any social event, and Tessa discovered that even outright rudeness did not always prevent people from attempting to wring from her every bit of information they suspected she might possess.

When Lady Frances and Letitia returned at the end of the following week, the news had already penetrated to the wilds of Pembrokeshire, and they were quite up-to-date on all details of the matter. Lady Frances spoke little of it outside her family, for she felt that to do so and still offer friendship to the Casters would be unconscionable. But neither she nor Tessa had the least influence on the behavior of Letitia, who used her former intimacy with Constance and her acquaintance with the Casters to draw to herself as much attention as she could.

Unforgivably, in Tessa's opinion, she even began to visit at the next house with great frequency, spending many hours commiserating with the dowager, who was glad enough of a sympathetic ear in which to pour out the expression of the wounds her unfeeling son caused her by his inconsideration in allowing himself to be taken in charge. Margaret, of course, saw through her, but for Tessa's sake, though the latter protested she should not do so, suffered her intrusion in silence. It was as well, for her mamma openly welcomed Letitia and she would have been powerless to prevent the visits. The only practical thing she could do was to tell the dowager as little as possible of what she knew of Jonathan's condition and circumstance. This at least made the tidbits that Letitia shamelessly garnered from her mother and then passed on to the eager ears of the ton of insignificant value. She did, however, confide most of this to Tessa, never guessing the value that her friend placed upon her every word.

It was nearly the end of March, and the season was at last getting fully under way, before the Lords finally sat in judgment on the most infamous member of their ranks. Letitia teased her father into obtaining for her a place in the visitors' gallery, but no amount of cajolery was sufficient to persuade her sister or mother to join her. She for her part utterly ignored their protests on her doing so and teased her reluctant betrothed into accompanying her in their stead.

Tessa flatly refused to discuss the matter even with those closest to her, feeling almost superstitious of the outcome if she so indulged herself. Nearly the only information she had of the trial, the scandal of which combined with the pomp of Lords had given it the appeal of a circus for most people, was from the libelous gossip of the newspapers and the morbid sensationalism of her sister's accounts. But although she refused to discuss the trial, the strain took its toll, literally sickening her, and frequently she felt too nauseous to eat.

Sir Edwin, as was usual with him, spoke little to his family of the work he was engaged in. At the beginning, though, he seemed rather amused, and he did comment that Astley's Circus was nothing to the spectacle of their lordships, but by the end of the first week of the trial, his expression was more often grim than humorous.

Tessa could not be certain that this spoke badly for Jonathan, but for the first time she forced herself to face up to the reality that Jonathan might not escape the duke's snare. She was too sensible to believe that her heart would break, but she knew that a future without him would stretch out as only a bleak prospect. In addition to this, a new anxiety beset her and made her snappish enough to cause comment in her family and among her friends. All in all, she was hard put to say whether it was more trying for her to worry about the trial or pretend that there was no need for her to do so.

Early in the second week of the trial, Sir Edwin came to her own room to ask for a private moment to speak with her. Tessa, who was putting the last touches to her dinner toilette, at once acquiesced, but an inner sense made her wary.

"Do you recall, Tess, any particular disturbance on the evening of your sister's betrothal ball?" he asked her at once.

"That is your barrister's voice, Papa," she said with an attempt at lightness. "You know there were no difficulties that night. What do you mean?"

"Selby," he said, speaking of the advocate whom he was up against, "came to me today in a private way. He doesn't like this mess, to be honest. He is doing what he must against Hartfield because that is his job, but he thinks the thing a farce and a miscarriage of justice, as do most in our profession.

"Gillane," he continued, "has been engineering his own investigation to assist the prosecution, and has turned up a man who may or may not be creditable. He claims he was a waiter here that night, sent over by the agency to assist our servants. He has said that he saw Hartfield come out into the hall in a murderous rage and that shortly afterward there were the sounds of a woman having hysterics coming from one of the anterooms. He also states that someone, he thinks a family member or connexion, had him fetch Lady Margaret to care for her sister-in-law! The man had no idea of the name of this woman, but Selby is well enough acquainted with you that even the vague description this man gave him was enough for him to believe that it was you he spoke of. Was it?"

Tessa could not deny this and saw no point in doing so. "Yes. Jonathan and Constance had an argument and she became quite upset and was about to make a scene, so I did what I could to prevent it."

"If you know that much, you must know some portion of what passed between them." He sighed and stood up from the chair in which he had been sitting. "I am sorry for this, Tess. I'd hoped Selby was mistaken or the man lying. I don't want you involved, but it is out of my hands; you will have to give testimony about that night."

Tessa was astounded. "But why? It is hardly a secret that the Hartfields did not get on and were known to argue frequently."

"Yes, but Selby and the duke feel this argument was significant because it took place only a very short time after Hartfield's return to town and they are convinced that there was something particular about the quarrels between them at this point and that to know the contents of the first one would be to know the motives and possibly even the guilt or innocence of Hartfield for certain."

While her father spoke, Tessa mentally reviewed what she remembered of that quarrel and knew that while in a way it would mean nothing for the contents of it to be known, it might also, as Jonathan

himself had suggested, seem as though his motive
for ridding himself of his wife was particularly potent.
This wasn't solid evidence, but all that was against
him was circumstantial, and in the end it was what
those that sat in judgment on him believed, not
what the facts were, that mattered. She managed to
fob her parent off with a vagueness about the night
in question, but if she were forced to testify under
oath, it would be an entirely different matter.

She was glad that the clannishness of the barristers had led Mr. Selby to warn her father of his
intentions of calling her to corroborate and improve
upon the information given by the waiter, but she
knew better than to trust it to the point of supposing
that Mr. Selby could be persuaded not to interview
her.

She teased herself so much with what she would
say and if evasion would serve to keep back the
truth, that by the time she sought her bed that
night, she had brought the migraine upon herself.
The next morning, though, brought her some degree
of comfort both physically and emotionally. The hint
of an idea had come into her aching head not long
before she had finally found sleep, and now, even
before the last mists of her rest had evaporated, it
came to fruition and her decision was as quick as it
was bold.

She washed and dressed with exceptional haste,
and took a tray in her room, requesting the town
carriage be made ready for her as soon as she was
done.

Colin McAffe, sunk deep in a brown study, sat
beside his cousin Tessa in the carriage as it rattled
over the rain-soaked streets. He moved to change
his position slightly, and the faint rustle of the paper
in his breast pocket made the reality of what they
were about more present. "I know you believe what
you are doing is right, Tess—" he began, but Tessa

had already heard his arguments through twice and was tired of listening politely.

"It is a necessity, Colin," she said shortly. "You know that, and to make me keep saying it is very discomfiting. Do you suppose I wish for a slapdash thing like this?"

"There are other solutions," he insisted.

"None of them tenable or practical," she said firmly. "This is the only course I can take, and if I suffer by it, at least I shall know that I was brought to it by no hand but my own."

"I don't think you can quite say that," Colin said waspishly, and at the darkling look she cast him, subsided into silence until the carriage rolled to a halt before the somber gates of one of the most dreaded places on earth. Newgate Prison.

The gatekeeper was unwashed and deaf enough that Colin had to come close to him and feel his fetid breath upon his cheek to make their purpose known. An appropriate number of coins changed hands, and in a few minutes they were inside the courtyard.

The portion of the prison to which they were led was not what Tessa had expected it to be and was in fact a rather special section set aside for special prisoners and the rare criminal who could well afford to purchase for himself luxury in the midst of his incarceration.

Tessa was heavily veiled, but she and her cousin, even dressed as plainly as possible, were more elegant than most who passed in those corridors, and they drew attention wherever they passed.

Colin handled all arrangements that were necessary for them to see Jonathan in his cell, and a fairly significant amount of the coin of the realm was used to ease their path. At last a man who was scant improvement over the gatekeeper came to fetch them into a less accessible portion of the building they were in, by leading them through a series of snaking corridors. Though the sights and smells of the place were hardly pleasant, Tessa was spared the vision of abject human misery which was most typical here, for Sir Edwin, even if he had failed Jonathan in other ways, had at the least seen to his comfort to the greatest extent that was manageable.

The place where Jonathan was being kept was a room off a dirt hallway which did not have the usual cell-like bars but was an actual room with an iron door that had only an iron grate at eye level and a smaller door cut into its center for food trays to be exchanged.

"Ye've visitors, milord," was the only warning Jonathan received that they were come; then the door swung open to reveal a room about the proportions of the dressing room he had hidden in at the Bellamys' house, but not nearly as well appointed.

The room did boast comforts that were unheard of in lesser parts of the prison; the Spartan furnishings were embellished by a small hearth and fire, several books on a table, and a bottle of wine and crusts of bread on a small pewter tray on a shelf. But though Tessa's mind absorbed these things as a whole, she saw none of it individually, for the sight of Jonathan commanded her full attention.

The amazement died out of his eyes, and his voice when he spoke was completely flat. "Why are you here?"

McAffe had been strictly admonished by his cousin to say nothing that was not required of him, keeping what opinions and objections he might have to himself until they were at least alone again. Therefore he stood beside Tessa in silence, his expression as bland as he could make it.

Nor did Tessa speak at first. Her eyes searched Jonathan for some visible signs of change, for the mark of suffering she was sure he must undergo in a place like this, but he was as well dressed and groomed as she had ever found him. There was no trace of gauntness or other signs of misery in his countenance, and if he seemed to her a trifle thinner, she conceded that this could be no more than her fancy. "I knew you would not like this," she said at last, her tone far cooler than she felt. "It is necessary, though. We shall have to speak before Colin. He came only because I gave him my pledge that I would not ask him to leave us and that I would go with him the moment the thing is accomplished."

Jonathan gave Colin a long unreadable look and then asked Tessa, "What is accomplished?"

As briefly as possible she told him of her interview with her father the evening before. "If only it had been one of our own servants that night," she concluded regretfully, "this difficulty would not even arise."

"You can't have come here to tell me this," Jonathan said, sounding a bit bemused. "Either Ryder or your father might have done that. Is it to ask me to free you from your promise to me? You need not have come to this noisome place for that; the claims of the oath you will take must supersede any I might have on you."

His voice was so completely emotionless that her heart nearly failed her. She began to fear that she had misread every loverlike thing she had noticed in him, harkening to her own wishes rather than his feelings. Taking her courage in both hands, she simply came out with it. "I am here to ask you to marry me. That is why it is necessary for Colin to be here. He obtained for us this morning a special license from the archbishop and will do so at once if you agree."

Jonathan's lips parted in complete astonishment. "You wish us to be married?" he asked, his voice soft with amazement. "Have you run mad or have I?"

This was hardly an encouraging response, but better than the withering scorn she knew him capable of and which was the worst she had feared. "Neither," she replied. "If I am your wife, I cannot testify against you."

He laughed with what sounded like genuine amusement. "My dear Tess, you completely astound me! All those half-pay officers resisted so that you might after all throw yourself away on an impoverished lord. Let me assure you, I am not worth it."

Tessa found she was forced to drop her eyes from his. "It is what I wish and . . . and also what is necessary." She glanced toward Colin, who was doing what he could to efface himself in a corner of the room. "I am sorry that what I have to say to you has to be said now and in this way, Jon, but it can't be helped. I need you to marry me, even if you do not particularly care for the scheme. I am increasing."

An absolute silence fell over the room, which lasted such a time that Tessa could no longer endure the wait for his reaction and raised her eyes. She found him regarding her.

"You may think that my name is better than none for your child," he said levelly, the shuttered expression in place and hiding from her any idea of what he felt, "but when you find yourself sharing my dishonor as well as my name, you may think differently. I am sure other solutions seem less palatable to you now than the easy one of our marriage, but you may well come to regret this choice."

"*I* shall not regret it," she said in a small but firm voice, and drawing a sustaining breath, added, "You refuse, then?"

"To meet my responsibilities?" he asked, and there was in his voice a hint of bitterness. "But how ungallant you must find me. As if I would find making you my wife a duty rather than a pleasure. You must forgive me, my love, this place seems to have had an unfortunate effect on my finer sensibilities. I have no thought to refuse for myself, but I think if I were of a stronger character, I might well do so for your sake."

"That would be no favor to me," Tessa told him plainly, and regretted her promise to Colin, for his presence was constraining, and she feared that Jonathan must find her cool indeed for the circumstances.

"You think so, do you?" responded Jonathan with soft sarcasm. "Well, we shall see. Why do you wait, priest?" he asked McAffe with a flicker of mockery. "The heavens are intent on decreeing the course of my life and want only one of their minions to seal the thing."

Colin took umbrage at his tone, as he had at most of the exchange that had taken place, but a glance from Tessa that was both plea and warning held his tongue, and fetching two guards to act as witnesses, he prepared to perform the marriage, which he mentally classified as the single most unwilling act of his entire ministry.

Chapter Six

Tessa returned home to face the second and in some ways more difficult portion of her scheme. Colin offered to accompany her through this stage as well, but she preferred to face the difficulty alone. Her first act was to find her father, who was fortunately at home, and then to summon her mother and sister as well. She had meant to tell them what she had done separately, but now felt she simply could not go through the strain of separate explanations. As it happened, though, only her mother was at home, Letitia having gone on an outing with her betrothed and some of their friends.

Tessa had already made up her mind to conceal her pregnancy from her family for as long as this was possible. She had not had her suspicions of this confirmed by the family's medical man, but she did not truly doubt it, and she knew perfectly well that they would all of them come to realize when at last they discovered her news that she had been breeding before the wedding had taken place. The truth was that at least in part she was craven; having sustained herself through her meeting and wedding to Jonathan, who she still had difficulty believing was now her husband after that brief, unemotional ceremony, she did not feel equal to any more complexity in her explanations for her behavior than she could avoid. In addition to this was the desire that Jonathan not cut too poor a figure in the matter and a very natural diffidence that any daughter must feel in admitting to a fond father that she has fallen from the path of virtue.

Tessa had never beheld two such totally astounded countenances. Her mother, who was *not* given to dramatizing herself, sought out her vinaigrette and could not entirely keep back the tears that started to her eyes. Her father's visage furrowed into a frown, and he questioned her motives and how she had gone about the thing in a cold, crisp manner that was nearly her undoing. But whether her parents would like or dislike the match, or the odd manner in which it was brought about, the important thing was that she was of age and the only way their displeasure could be practically expressed was in the withholding of their emotional or financial support. But Tessa knew and loved her family too well to imagine for even a moment that either thing would occur.

From the tenor of her father's questions she knew he had guessed at their clandestine meetings, but he could not persuade her to confirm his suspicions without speaking openly before his wife, and he allowed the thing to drop. Lady Frances, when she had got over the shock of the thing, accepted without question Tessa's assurances that it was during the time that she had spent at Caster House before their visit at Boxwood that the attachment had begun, and accepted equally that they had intended to wait until he was cleared and a proper time had passed to marry, and had only decided on doing the thing in this way after Sir Edwin had told Tessa that she would need to testify against Jonathan.

But if Sir Edwin did not believe her, by the time an hour had passed and all explanations and exclamations had been exhausted, he took his daughter's hands in his. "I can't say I care for this match. Hartfield as a man I find unexceptionable and gladly welcome him as my son-in-law. I do not even mind his want of fortune. It is his misfortune, not his fault that his father had a taste for speculation and cards. If you are satisfied that he makes this match for more than your dowry, then so shall I be. But given the sensationalism that surrounds him, I cannot but feel that you have acted in haste, and probably unnecessarily."

"What was the point in waiting a few months, when our wedding now could mean helping him?" Tessa asked.

"Though I was concerned for Hartfield in this, my chief concern was to spare you involvement," he told her. "Even given a better understanding of his motive, I don't believe their lordships would convict him. I'll do what I can now to keep you from it entirely. I'll see Selby tonight and tell him of this, though it will certainly make him stare, and I think that there will never be a question of your name being brought up. If the waiter testifies, it will only concern an unknown woman, for Selby believes he has no idea of your identity."

Reassured by this, Tessa felt lightened by at least one burden. She embraced her father and thanked him for his acceptance of her choice, which she felt was done with more understanding than she had hoped for.

"I want you happy, Tess," he said gently. "You are a sensible young woman and old enough to know your mind. If you are content with the matter, then I shall attempt to content myself as well."

Lady Frances had sat musingly through their exchange and now spoke ruminatively. "This is not going to be the easiest thing to carry off in the ton, Tess. It would be easier if you were not also a great heiress, as was his first wife. You have surely thought yourself what people will say."

"They will be mistaken," Tessa said firmly.

"That is all very well, but they will still say things," Lady Frances said. "What happens otherwise must depend on the outcome of Lord Hartfield's trial and the way that people view the verdict. If he is acquitted and the sympathy is with him, then you should come through the gossip mill relatively unscathed except for a few bruises from the hurly-burly way you went about your wedding and the fact that it took place when he is supposedly in mourning for his first wife. Though it *is* more than six months, and given the circumstances, no one could surely expect more than the shortest period that strict decency demands."

"We will not, I think," put in Sir Edwin, "let the precise date of the wedding be known, and certainly never the place of it."

Tessa sat again beside her mother on the sofa and listened without comment as her parents worked out the best manner of putting forth the news so that the young couple would suffer the least from the censure and vagaries of society. It was decided that no announcement would be made until after the trial and (hopefully) acquittal of Jonathan. The dowager marchioness and Lady Margaret would be told, of course, and firmly impressed that they would be doing the Hartfields a great disservice if the news was made public too swiftly.

Sir Edwin suggested that Jonathan and Tessa might do best to take their honeymoon at Boxwood, not returning to town until the little season at best or even not until next spring, when it might be supposed that any talk would have long since died away. Tessa supposed that this is what they would do, but surprisingly, Lady Frances advised against this.

"I think it would be best to do the thing with

panache rather than going off into seclusion as if there were something to do penance for," she insisted. "If Hartfield is to give up his mourning, then they should go into society at once. Not every couple has a wedding journey and a honeymoon. Some send out cards at once that they are receiving their visits of ceremony."

Tessa smiled ruefully. "Suppose we are to be outcast and no one comes?"

"Oh, they will come," Lady Frances said with cynical assurance. "In fact, if all is well for Hartfield, I suspect you shall find yourself lionized. Your marriage may have about it a faint aura of the disreputable, but the very fact of it is quite unique, and society always loves the unique, especially when it is amongst its own. The only restriction I think you would be wise to follow would be to forgo dancing until the year is up. That doesn't mean you may not attend balls, but you must be content at them with cards or conversation."

Tessa was unsure of the idea, but was at the least intrigued by it. She had already envisioned that their first days or even weeks together might be tended by a bit of awkwardness and she was not loath to spend some of her time with him in the company of others as well until they had learned an easy footing with each other in their altered circumstances. She neither agreed nor disagreed with her mother now. "I must consult Jon's wishes," was all that she said, "for this has been an ordeal for him and he may wish for the peace and quiet of Boxwood."

The only thing that went forward from Lady Frances' idea was the decision that should Jonathan decide to go with her scheme, it might be best if they set up their own establishment as soon as possible. Sir Edwin pledged his clerk to look into houses that might remain for hire for the season, though the most choice locations were undoubtedly already snatched up.

There was then the discreet mention by Tessa of the best way that Letitia might learn of her news. If Lady Frances was closer to her younger daughter than her elder, she also was aware of Letitia's short-comings and knew that she was bound to take the information that her unmarried and therefore unre-markable sister was now not only wed, and before her, but wed to a man of greater rank than she herself had lured into parson's mousetrap. Sir Edwin, as might be expected, divorced himself from the proceedings at this point and Lady Frances, know-ing that she would probably be the best to handle the matter in any case, took the unwanted task to herself.

It was as well that she did. To say that Letitia was upset and infuriated by the news would be a master-piece of understatement. When she was told later that day, her immediate response was to cast two statuettes one after the other into the grate, dashing them to pieces. Then, after uttering several animad-versions on the character of her sister, she burst into tears that might easily have become hysterical if Lady Frances had not been familiar with the way to deal with them.

When Letitia had at last been restored to a degree of calm, Lady Frances advised her to be sensible, for her fury would change nothing and if she presented such a face on the matter to the world it could well be that *she* ended up condemned as a jealous cat.

Letitia took this statement surprisingly well. "I am hardly jealous of poor Tess," she said condescend-ingly. "I am sure that she has done the best she could to find herself a proper husband, not that this one is so proper. Oh, it will be such a scandal, Mamma, and how will that be for my wedding? If Tess has placed herself beyond the pale, then no one will come to my wedding breakfast!"

Tears welled up in Letitia's lovely eyes, and Lady Frances patted her hand and said bracingly, "That need not be a worry, I think. I have already reassured Tess that if I know anything of these matters, they are more likely to be courted for their odd circumstances."

"*That* is just splendid," Letitia said bitingly, and unblushingly changing her ground, added, "Everyone will be making so much of a fuss over Tess that my wedding will be completely ignored."

Loving mother that she was, there were times when even Lady Frances found Letitia less than easy to deal with. "Your wedding is a full two months off, Letty. By then I am sure Jonathan and Tessa will have settled into their usual roles in the world and no one will give them a thought on your wedding day."

"They are doing so now," Letitia snapped. "I suppose Tess may marry where she pleases, but she did not have to do so now. It would have been more proper for her to have waited until next September in any case. I know she has done this thing just to spite me for reminding her that she would no longer have precedence over me, and she has wed a marquis that I might be cast in the shade. Hartfield, of all people," she added, stamping her foot. "I wish her well of him. I only hope it may not come to her ending as Constance did, for Hartfield is remaining true to form in carrying off yet another heiress under the noses of her family and society. She had better have a care not to vex him as Connie did."

But Lady Frances would not have talk such as this even from her beloved daughter. She called Letitia sharply to order and forbade her ever to say such a thing again to anyone, at risk of her severe and probably irrevocable displeasure. Perceiving that she had gone too far, Letitia subsided and begged pardon, contenting herself with only one or two pithy comments on the lures of fortune hunters and the gullibility of some heiresses.

*   *   *

Jonathan's trial before Lords lasted until the end of that same week. In spite of assurances from Sir Edwin that their anxiety need not extend beyond a healthy concern, Tessa, and indeed all those who had Hartfield's welfare at heart, felt that week as the longest of their lives. In generalities, the probabilities were ceaselessly discussed, but in specifics, voices became hushed as if superstitious of saying too much aloud. The tension and suspense of the wait for the outcome of the trial were tangible things.

When the hoped-for, yet dreaded verdict came at last, ringing out through the court, it was found that the vote of their lordships was not unanimous for acquittal, but it was the majority opinion by a healthy margin. Jonathan Hartfield had been able to stand firm against the spite, money, and influence of the Duke of Gillane.

A great number of the lords insisted on shaking Jonathan's hand as the trial was adjourned, and though he was emotionally exhausted, he heeded the advice of his new father-in-law and submitted with good humor and grace to the goodwill of his fellows.

Sir Edwin stood a little apart from the throng about Jonathan, reflecting that his wife's good social sense was proved yet again. If he was any judge of the matter, by the time their lordships had returned to their families, their good opinion of Hartfield would be spread throughout the ton and the pendulum of popular opinion would swing again, this time firmly in Jonathan's favor. The very people who had cut him a few months ago, Sir Edwin supposed, would now declare to their fellows that it was shocking to think that a peer of the realm could be pilloried for no worse a crime than having a faithless wife who had mistaken the strength of her sleeping draught.

Having a mind to the anxiety of Tessa and the others, Sir Edwin motioned to a servant, and hastily writing on the back of one of his visiting cards, had the message sent to his home at once that Jonathan had been acquitted and that they could both be expected in a short while.

The message was received at the Bellamy house with unanimous joy, but at least some of those present in the house felt a lingering concern. Having been warned by Sir Edwin that this day would probably see the matter out, the Caster ladies joined with the Bellamys to await the news in the hope that the presence of each would divert the others. It was a vain hope. Lady Frances did what she could, but even she found herself a bit anxious and not at her best as a hostess. Tessa was, as usual, outwardly in command of herself, but her quietness gave away her anxiety to those who knew her well; Letitia, who continued to vent her resentment of her sister in small snipping ways, was sullen and sarcastic, making statements about fortune hunters as broad as she dared before her mother and the other ladies. Lady Margaret, who did not want for understanding despite her quiet ways, was made acutely uncomfortable by this and the fear that she and her mother were actually being wished at Jericho by the others, and was conscious of the fact that her mother's chatter must be even more grating to those who were not accustomed to it. The dowager, for her part, was the only woman relatively untroubled, and the only one who reiterated constantly how overset her nerves were, but as her complexion was robust and her spirits unflagging, this went unheeded, as did her complaints on her children's total lack of consideration.

Tessa thought the waiting interminable, but when a carriage was at last heard to stop in the street in front of the house, and Letitia had run to the window to confirm the arrival of her father and Jonathan, a sudden clutching feeling inside of her made her wish for a bit more time before having to face her husband for the first time since their wedding. She was not certain whether she was sorry or glad that this meeting would take place in a room full of people.

In the end she was glad of it. As soon as he stood on the threshold of the room, her eyes flew to his, and when she found no reassurance there, dropped away. Tessa would have been amused at the suggestion that she was in any way shy; unquestionably the young woman who had met him secretly in the quiet of the night and who had boldly sought his lovemaking could not be thought diffident. But the Tessa who had braved the horrors of Newgate to insist on their marriage and the one who waited in silent dread for the rejection by the one person whose regard meant everything to her were not at all the same woman. Forced by events to be introspective of late, she supposed it was because she had reached the point where she had pushed the relationship as far as she could toward success, and now it must be his turn to wish for it. Her fear was that she had pushed too far and that he was not willing for it to go any further.

Jonathan was at once set upon by his mother, who fell upon his neck and declared that her senses had scarcely borne the tensions of this day. Lady Margaret was next to go to him, and after that her parents vied for his attention and even Letitia looked for his notice. Tessa had risen at his entrance but stood a little apart from the rest; her appearance was one of cool command, her manner a bit detached. This was, of course, merely her first line of defense against her fears that he was come to her out of duty rather than choice, but her husband, weary and anxious in his own right, was not as perceptive as he might have otherwise been and noticed only the want of especial warmth when at last she welcomed him home. Neither allowed for the situation, and both were more on guard in each other's presence than they had ever been before.

Feeling that one chapter in the lives of dear ones

had at last been closed, Lady Frances brightened perceptibly as she looked forward to the next, which she thought might just be rather exciting. Rallying to the situation, she managed to muzzle her sharp-tongued daughter, and maneuvered the Caster ladies into returning to their own home until it was time for them to return for the celebratory dinner that evening. She informed her husband that he was definitely required on her expedition to Rundell & Bridge, the most exclusive of jewelers, to select a diamond-and-ruby pendant to be worn at Letitia's wedding.

It had been decided for practical reasons that Tessa and Jonathan would do better to stay in her father's house until they had agreed on a suitable place to hire for themselves. Lady Frances had noticed the want of ease in the brief exchange between Tessa and her husband, and to ease any further awkwardness, she had Jonathan shown to his room first, on the suggestion that he might wish to rest before dinner, and thought of a perfect reason why Tessa should remain downstairs with her for a time. At last, though, her manipulation could go no further and she was forced to leave the couple to their own devices. Kissing her daughter on the cheek and enigmatically bidding her to have patience, she left with her husband for the city.

Tessa's bedchamber had again been moved, this time to quite the other side of the house so that they might have rooms which adjoined through a common sitting room. When Tessa at last went upstairs, it was to this shared room that she went. She was genuinely surprised when she entered it and found Jonathan encased in a comfortable chair clearly awaiting her.

"Well, madam wife, alone at last," he said lightly, "but privacy doesn't have the same romance, does it, in the light of day, when quite legal and respectable. Perhaps we should take turns locking ourselves in our bedchambers for days at a time and visiting each other with great stealth to make love in the moonlight."

She was a bit disconcerted by his reference to their lovemaking, but managed to reply in kind. "We may do so if *you* choose to be locked up again, for I should hate it." Then, realizing that his recent incarceration in Newgate made her words insensitive, she added, "But you have had enough of it to last a lifetime, I suppose, so it is unkind of me to say so."

"I don't doubt it is a mistake to attempt to relive the past in any event," he said. "One must have memories, of course, but should avoid repetition."

"Even of the good things?" she asked quizzically, and sat near to him.

He gave her a very long look before replying, "There is danger, I think, in repetition. One ought to be satisfied with memory, though there is nothing the matter with doing things in the present to make a memory. We, for example, should have cast McAffe from my cell and made wild love on my cot. Now, that would be a romantic thing to remember, or at least an original thing."

Tessa smiled, but not even his deliberate lightness could overcome her feeling of discomfort. "You talk nonsense, my lord."

"Well, we must talk something," he said with a sigh that was at least half-exasperated. " 'Original' is just a nice word for 'peculiar,' and that is what our marriage is," he said plainly. "But it would be foolish to refine too much on the disadvantages of our beginning when there is much to be said for the advantages—the first and foremost is that I am here and not on Tyburn Tree. I was startled and a bit to confused by the swiftness of your hand to properly thank you for what you have done for me. Sir Edwin has told me that your testimony would hardly have convicted me, but on the other hand, you clearly did not confide in him the extent of your knowledge, so who can truly say? In any event, I don't want the truth known to the world, so I thank you most sincerely."

His gratitude was the very last thing she wanted, for it put him in a position of petitioner and her of conferrer and set a breach between them. "That was a part of my reason for wishing us married, but hardly the first one," she began.

But he spoke again before she could go on. "Yes, of course, how selfish of me to think so! Your consideration must of course be first. I am truly sorry for that, Tess. I never meant for that last night to happen, and certainly not for you to suffer in the outcome."

Never had Tessa had more need for her self-possession and never had it more completely deserted her. Everything she said seemed to elicit the wrong response from him, making her feel less and less secure of him and of herself. "You hardly seduced me," she said a bit gruffly.

"Yes, I did," he replied with one of his sudden smiles. "I think I first planned it the night of Letty's betrothal ball. You were so self-possessed, but I thought I surprised a hint of admiration in your eyes. I am shockingly vain, am I not? I don't suppose I should have done so in the normal way of events; gently bred maidens are not truly my style— my reputation is for being a cold fish, not a loose one."

"I don't think you are either."

"No?" he said, laughing. "That is surprising, but good I think. Then I won't take full blame for our situation, if you please. By the end of the first sennight I was as certain as I could be that my feelings were reciprocated, and that, of course, combined with the forced intimacy of our visits, rather made the thing inevitable." He paused for a brief moment and then went on, "I hope you don't think I mean this to be a true marriage of convenience. Our two-month separation has not lessened the attraction—at least for me."

These words were the most gratifying she had heard him speak, but they brought to her cheeks a most unaccustomed blush. "Nor for me," she admitted, forcing herself to meet his eyes.

She was sitting on a striped silk sofa, one of a pair in the room and he got up and came over beside her. He took her in his arms and kissed her long and longingly until she withdrew a little away from him. It was only that she wished to see his expression, that she might guess how much of his desire was for her as a woman and how much for her as a person. But he stiffened momentarily at her withdrawal and moved back from her a bit, giving her one of his speculative looks that so had the power to nonplus her.

"You aren't going to surprise me by turning out to be daytime prudish, are you?" he said suspiciously. "We *shall* have problems, then, for I fear my appetites are not so well-regulated."

The idea that he could suspect her of any manner of prudery after the wanton way she had gone to his bed and forced his hand in marriage greatly amused her. For the first time she laughed with genuine warmth and disclaimed any likelihood of *that* being one of their difficulties.

He dropped his eyes for a moment, and when he looked up again, they were completely serious. "I hope we shall have very few difficulties, Tess. One of the worst of the problems between Connie and me was that we were at odds over small things from the outset and were never quite able to reconcile our petty disagreements before they grew into large and bitter quarrels. I am not yet certain what manner of bargain we have made with each other, but I want it to be honest from the very beginning. It is for better or worse, and not to do everything to make the best of it is not a mistake that I would care to repeat.

There are so many similarities in our matching to my first marriage that I find it nearly frightening, but the outcome needn't be the same if we start as we mean to go on."

It was this speech that Tessa found dismaying, such a far cry was it from the declarations of love she so wanted to hear. "Start as you mean to go on" was very good advice, she supposed, but she simply could not bring herself to say to him the loving words on her own lips. She cursed her own want of romance for tying her tongue; this one excursion into its realm was so unique to her that she did not know how to properly proceed when she felt so great a risk of rejection and was so fearful of it. So she simply agreed with him and gave him no more hint of her true feelings than he had given her of his.

In a while he did go to his room to rest before dinner, a family event to which neither looked forward. Each would have preferred a quiet private evening, but the happiness and pleasure of the rest of the family at the happy outcome of Jonathan's difficulties was quite infectious, and Jonathan, weary and disinclined to discuss his ordeal though he was, found the evening more enjoyable than he had supposed he would. Tessa, still unsure of how willingly he welcomed her as his wife, took her lead from him and was persuaded to let go of some of her concern.

Lady Frances thoughtfully kept the evening short, and once again managed to tactfully herd the Caster ladies to an early departure. An evening of enjoyable conversation and good wine had mellowed most of any awkwardness left between Jonathan and Tessa, and when he accompanied her, not to their sitting room, but to her own bedroom, Tessa felt little diffidence in his company and allowed herself to be enfolded in his arms in the most natural way.

She had thought she could not forget the feeling of his lips on hers, but the sweetness of the sensation poured over her like a warm silky bath. There was no impatience for each other this time, in spite of their separation. Each knew that this night, and indeed the endless nights stretching before them, would bring all the physical delights and fulfillment that either could wish for. This night was a night for exploring and wonder, for savoring and discovery.

When at last their appetites were slaked and Tessa lay quietly in the arms of her sleeping husband, tiny tendrils of anxiety again found their way into her thoughts. This was all so much better than she had dared to hope it would be, and yet . . . Men, she knew, were different creatures; desire for him might not be synonymous with love, as it was for her. She supposed that since her usually glib tongue could not be relied upon in this situation, she would have to bide her time and let his behavior speak his feelings and trust to herself to read him aright.

Chapter Seven

The marriage in which Tessa and Jonathan found themselves linked was not precisely an unhappy state of affairs, but neither was it particularly happy. After that first afternoon and evening together, the constraint between them vanished and they returned to a footing much like they had enjoyed before he had gone to Newgate. They were unquestionably becoming good friends, they were already eager lovers, but any soft words of love that might have attended their growing intimacy remained unspoken. Tessa despaired that they ever would be and did her best to resign herself to this. Jonathan seemed so completely unrestrained with her that she could not but believe that he was being completely open with her in his feelings and that he never showed her the full depth for the simple reason that there wasn't any.

So she affected a light manner, much like his own toward her, with just that shading of distance that would protect her from any suspicion that she had a heart to be wounded. It was not so much that she feared he would be deliberately unkind to her if he knew that she was in love with him; he was far too much a gentleman to behave in that manner. Moreover, she thought even cruelty would be far more bearable than the accidental bruisings which would be the inevitable result of his indifference.

Beyond this there was only one thing that marred the smooth surface of their growing relationship, and that was her money. Tessa did not suppose that he had deliberately married her for her money as she supposed he had Constance, but she knew that for a man in his position it must signify to some degree. She could not know to what degree this was true and did not wish to know, but she did discover that he was sensitive to the label of fortune hunter. Indeed, a thinly veiled remark of Letitia's to this effect elicited from him a smoothly spoken but quite nasty response.

Letitia did not present the problem her sister had feared she would. Her exchange with Jonathan had taken place on the second day of his being in the house, and though he had given Letitia no cause for overt offense, she was wary of the edge of his tongue after that. Tessa also noted that Letitia seemed to be of two minds about Jonathan. On the one hand she would occasionally give him the same darkling looks of resentment that she usually reserved for her sister, and on the other it was clear that Letitia could not quite help admiring him.

If Tessa was not romantically inclined, Letitia was overly so, and given all that Jonathan had been through and even the odd circumstances of his marriage to Tessa, he was certainly a figure of romance. Dangerous men have always had their appeal for innocent and gently bred females, and Letitia was no exception to this rule. Therefore there were times when she flirted with Jonathan like a moth to the flame. Moreover, Lord Torrance was plainly jealous at any hint of her dallying with her brother-in-law, and Letitia fairly basked in the added attention this brought from her betrothed.

Jonathan was not ignorant of her motives, and

though he did not particularly like his sister-in-law, he was not above indulging in a little self-amusement. He did not play up to her flirtation in the usual way, for to do so in the presence of his wife and her family would have been foolish beyond permission. But when he could manage the thing so that he gave no offense there, and at the same time make Torrance, whom he did not dislike but who bored him to distraction, rise to the proffered bait, he did not resist the temptation.

He was not entirely successful, though, in keeping this reprehensible amusement from his wife. She might not have heard their exchanges, but she saw the viscount's stormy mien and the high color in her sister's cheeks and drew her own conclusions. This did not really upset or concern her. Letitia was beautiful. All men flirted with her—Tessa doubted they were able to help themselves. She might have blamed Letitia for her arch glances of encouragement, but one might as well blame fire for burning when it was touched.

Nevertheless, she was glad that Jonathan had fallen in with Lady Frances' idea for them to go into society at once, as it meant that they would soon be starting their own life apart from that of her family. The notice was sent to all the fashionable papers the same day that Jonathan returned, and the following morning more than one paper fell into the porridge through fingers rendered nerveless with astonishment. It would not have been proper for the world to call upon them until they made it known that they were receiving, but anyone who could otherwise think of a reason to call at either the Bellamy house or the Caster house without being awkward over Hartfield's recent ordeal or openly curious about his latest escapade made quite a point of doing so. Little more than simple fact was gleaned from the Bellamys, a few more interesting tidbits were to be had from the dowager, but there was absolutely no one who was able to discover just when or where this incredible wedding had taken place, and this was due to the fact that outside of Sir Edwin and Lady Frances, Colin McAffe and the Hartfields themselves, no one knew of it.

This was the most delicate part of her scheme, Lady Frances confided to her daughter; it was now that society would either take offense at their boldness or admire them for it. Perhaps because the tide of opinion still ran high in Jonathan's favor so soon after his acquittal, there was not even the need for an anxious moment. The news that the Hartfields would soon be setting up their own household to remain in town for the season was met with marked interest and Lady Frances hadn't any doubt that they would soon be receiving far more invitations than they could possibly manage to accept.

Sir Edwin's clerk had found three eligible houses for them to look at. The one on Upper Mount Street, though not the most elegant address, exactly suited both Jonathan and Tessa and the lease was signed by the middle of the week. It was suitably furnished and ready to be lived in at once, but Tessa could not quite like the hangings and other minor domestic arrangements. Rather than move there and be in the middle of a fuss while the redecoration was seen to, Tessa and Jonathan decided that it would be best to remain with her parents for the fortnight this would take to accomplish.

"I think," began Lady Frances one afternoon over luncheon, "that you should begin receiving by Monday, even though it must be here rather than in Upper Mount Street. I have an idea that it would be thought behindhand in your papa and me if we do not make some special notice of your marriage despite the delicacy of Jonathan's being in mourning."

"You can scarcely give them a grand ball, as you did at my betrothal," Letitia said quickly, for it would not suit her at all for Tessa to be saluted in so grand a manner as to make her own wedding anticlimactic.

"Of course not," Lady Frances said a bit tartly. Dearly as she loved Letitia, she was beginning to find the younger girl decidedly tiresome. "But that does not mean we may not put forward some sort of entertainment in their honor. I think we should plan it for just before you remove from here, Tess. That will give us time to prepare and send out the invitations and make your transition back to society quite smooth."

Tessa agreed, but Jonathan said in his quiet way that was so difficult to read, "I wish, Beaumère, that you will not feel obliged to make a great deal of us. You have more than enough to occupy your time and energies with Letty's wedding plans."

"You would dislike it, then?" Tessa asked, not presuming his meaning.

"No," he admitted, "but your mamma and papa have done so very much for us already that I would not care to ask more than was reasonable or than simple gratitude could repay."

This speech did her son-in-law no disservice in Lady Frances' eyes. She did dislike the bother of planning their social responsibilities, and of late, with one thing and another, she had not been able to lean on Tessa as she had in the past. She resumed her duties reluctantly, but not unwillingly except for now and again when she felt her efforts unappreciated. That Jonathan should recognize the generosity of her offer assured that she would put her best effort into the scheme.

"As if a simple reception to launch you into the world as a couple could signify!" she said with a delighted laugh. "When will the house be ready for you? Friday, I think you told me. Very well, we shall send out cards for Thursday night."

The Hartfields began receiving that next Monday and the callers began almost too early to be decent, but they were prepared for a possible onslaught and Jonathan remarked by Wednesday that a party in their honor was now quite unnecessary; so many people filled the drawing room each morning that three receptions had in effect already been held and the one on the following night could only be repetitious.

Tessa dressed with even more than her usual care for her first appearance in society as a married woman. She wore a silk gown of her favorite cornflower blue and sapphires in her ears and at her throat. Although she had chosen her uncomplex hairstyle not only because it was most becoming but also because it was simple, now, as she regarded herself in her looking glass, she wished she had long hair to pin up in an elegant style. This, though, was her only self-complaint. She knew she looked very well, which since she knew she would never be beautiful, satisfied her. In addition to the flattering lines and color of her gown, she was now permitted, as a married woman, more latitude in the area of makeup, and she had blackened her lashes and applied a faint touch of rouge to her cheeks, and felt, quite absurdly, she knew, that she was at last completely grown-up.

A number of aunts and uncles and a few bosom cronies of her parents had been invited to dinner before the reception, and these were the first to formally wish the young couple happy. Dinner went off exceptionally well, given the company, which Letitia maintained was "the greatest selection of bores ever assembled." But as these same bores were expected to do handsomely by her in their bride gifts, she made herself agreeable to everyone and thereby regained the fond opinion of her mother, which had been absent for most of the last fortnight.

Dinner was ended, the receiving line with its commonplace repetitions was at last dispersed, and Tessa decided that she had done and said everything that was proper to one evening and now might please herself. This was principally accomplished by seeking out the company of her cousin Colin, whom she had seen very little of since the day he had accompanied her to Newgate.

He was found, as was not uncommon, in the center of a group of young matrons and dowagers who were attracted by his exceptional looks, yet, assuming his high moral tone, found in him a measure of safety. Tessa bore him off from under their noses in masterly style.

"Taking the shine out of our Letty tonight, aren't you?" he said with a smile when they had discovered an uncrowded corner in which to sit. "I must think your marriage agrees with you."

Tessa laughed. "Perhaps, but I suspect it is only the paint."

"Paint!" he cried with mock horror. "Wanton woman. I must say I never would have guessed. Whatever you've done, it looks natural enough."

"It wasn't likely that I would deck myself out as haymarket ware," she said caustically. "A married woman is given license to wear it, but cannot wear it with license."

"Constance wore paint, and you *could* tell," Colin said.

"Constance did a lot of things she shouldn't have, and one could tell," Tessa said waspishly. "If you think that I have done this to ape her, you are fair and far off. She was beautiful and elegant and I haven't the smallest wish to invite comparison to her; I should not at all care for the manner in which I would come off."

Colin was a bit surprised by her attack. "It was only a comment," he said defensively, "but if you think there is anything you can do to avoid comparisons, it is you who are 'fair and far off.' "

"I know," Tessa said with a rueful sigh. "But I wish to minimize them as much as possible."

"I know one thing you might do," Colin said helpfully. "Be different enough in your own way to make people notice you without thinking of Constance. Cut a dash, Tess! You've said yourself that married women have more latitude."

"Constance certainly cut a dash."

"Being brazen and available is not at all the same thing," Colin said dryly.

Tessa laughed, but admonished him as well. "Your want of charity is showing again."

"It is not my want of charity that you see," Colin said haughtily, "it is my absolute honesty. I think you should be daring, not brazen; you have good coloring, a fine figure, and excellent carriage. I fancy there are extremes of style that would become you rather a lot."

"Which extremes?" she asked suspiciously.

"I don't know. You would have to go to all the best modistes and milliners and discover that," he answered. "What I am saying is that you have the face and form, the self-possession and panache to carry anything off. Don't ape the styles, Tess, set them."

"I am as likely to set myself up as a figure of fun," she said, unconvinced.

He shook his head, smiling. "Not in the least. You have the spirit for it as well. Be brave, Tess. I don't think you'll regret it."

Their *tête-à-tête* was brought to an end by the arrival of Jonathan to disturb their seclusion. With smooth but scant apology to McAffe, he bore his wife off to meet with one he termed quite his favorite cousin, but when Tessa was presented to the woman, she distinctly recalled that Jonathan had mentioned her name before and in not nearly so favorable a way. She had a small glimmering suspicion that he had interrupted her and Colin quite deliberately, but she could think of no cause for this but jealousy, and this was completely absurd, because she had told him once already Colin was as a brother to her.

The remainder of the evening passed off pleasantly and quickly. Almost before she was aware of it, the clock had struck three and the last of the guests was being escorted to the door. Jonathan kissed her lightly when they went up to bed, and suggested that they not concern themselves with rising early to remove to their new house in the morning, and Tessa readily agreed. When she was finally undressed and in bed, she reviewed the evening with great pleasure. If her marriage was not the ideal she could wish it, she had to admit that she was exceptionally content in it. And that, she supposed, must be enough for her. So untroubled was she that she closed her eyes on that thought and in the next moment was completely asleep.

An early remove to Upper Mount Street proved to be out of the question in any case. Nearly everything but the last of their personal belongings had already been placed in the house, but Tessa, enumerating for her mother at breakfast the preparatory arrangements she had made for their imminent habitation, was informed by that lady of several tasks she had left undone. Tessa was inclined to regard these details as minor, but Lady Frances insisted that Tessa would be glad soon enough that she had heeded her mother's advice and went as far as to offer to assist her so that all might be accomplished by after luncheon at the latest.

Tessa was in this way persuaded to agree, and Jonathan when appealed to admitted that he did not mind in the least delaying their residency in Upper Mount Street by a few more hours.

Sir Edwin, who rose early no matter what his hour of retirement, had left for his chambers, and Letitia,

declining an offer to join her mother and sister,
declared that she would just walk over to Hookam's
to exchange the novel she had been reading. This
left Jonathan alone in the house, but it suited him,
for he had legal matters to attend to, pertaining to
some small investments he had made the previous
year.

Letitia, though, did not go to Hookam's: she did
not even have a book on loan at the moment. She
returned to her room, ostensibly to change for the
streets, but she sat at her dressing table to finalize
the plotting of a plan that had been in her head for
nearly a sennight.

She was self-centered enough to genuinely suppose that to some degree her sister had embarked on
her marriage to put her nose out of joint, and though
as her mother had said, there was nothing that could
be done about it now, she fully intended to pay her
sister out if the opportunity presented itself, and she
believed it had.

It did not occur to Letitia that Jonathan could have
any motive for the attention he paid her beyond
attraction to herself. There were moments when she
suspected his attitude was faintly mocking, but other
admirers had used this device to fascinate, and she
thought no more of it than that.

Nor did Letitia doubt that Jonathan had had any
motive for wedding Tessa other than her fortune.
Tessa was always the one in the family heralded for
her intelligence and good sense, and Letitia could
only wonder at first how she had after all let herself
be taken in by a fortune hunter. But simple, careful
observation told her that Tessa was most attracted to
her husband, maybe even a little in love with him.
Letitia did not look to see if these sentiments were
returned, for that would have been incompatible
with her belief that it was secretly she whom Hartfield
preferred.

Her feelings for Jonathan were mixed, but they in

no way deterred her from the course she meant to take. She might generally jealously guard her admirers from poaching, but she thought it worthwhile to cast this one off herself if in the end it would help to remove the scales from her sister's eyes. For this was the way she was viewing the matter to salve her own conscience. It was for Tessa's own good that she should know Jonathan did not care a fig for her beyond her dowry, yet at the same time it would serve the purpose of showing to Tessa that her grand match made in haste to usurp her own position was not so grand a bargain after all.

Ever since her plan had taken nebulous form, she had been waiting for the opportunity to find her brother-in-law alone. She had nearly despaired of it by this point, but fate had been kind at last. She had heard him tell her mother that he meant to work in the bookroom, and after a careful glance into her mirror to assure herself that she was in looks today, she descended to the ground floor to find him there. Letitia entered the room with confidence, believing completely that she could lure Jonathan into an outward show of his attraction to her; then Tessa need only be informed of his perfidy and made to see that she had quite brought it on herself.

Jonathan was sitting at her father's desk writing when she came into the room. He was absorbed in his work and she moved so quietly that she startled him when she came up beside him. She greeted him by almost speaking in his ear, which made him jump. She had spoken huskily to arouse his interest from the start, but all she succeeded in doing was discomposing him and annoying him for interrupting his work.

"I didn't know you were in, Letty," he said brusquely.

"I decided that I did not wish for another predictable gothic romance from Hookam's," she explained languidly. "I am sure I may find something far more edifying right here."

He gave her a brief smile. "I have no doubt of it," he replied amiably. He glanced down at his work again, but Letitia did not take the hint that he wished to be back to his work, so he continued, "I hope I shan't disturb your search, Letty. Please just go on as if I weren't here. I shall be done shortly."

This was not a response that Letitia had looked for, but she was far from daunted. She moved over to the shelves of books that lined the walls and pretended to be absorbed in their titles for several minutes.

"Jonathan," she called to him presently. "There are several here that seem most interesting and I can't seem to make up my mind. Could you help me to choose? Tessa had told me that you are quite bookish, so I know I may trust your advice."

"Trust rather your taste," he advised, looking up from his work. But he saw that she continued to regard him expectantly, and suppressing a sigh, he rose and went over to her.

When she pointed out the titles to him, he was frankly amazed. They were books of serious history and meditation that he would have supposed would have killed her with boredom. A flickering suspicion came into his head, but he responded to her blandly, telling her what she wished to know of each as far as he was able.

Letitia moved very close to him to point out yet another volume. "I fancy my Walter never reads anything more enlightening than the *Sporting News*," she said wistfully. "I cannot help but admire a man who has developed his mind as well as his form. There are those who would benefit from your example, I think."

The caressing note in her voice brought his suspicions into flame. "Is that a compliment to me or a criticism of Torrance?" he quizzed her gently. He had no motive, not even self-amusement, for dallying with her now, but he had no wish to offend her, either, by dealing with her as summarily as he wished to do.

"Walter is not a stupid man," she said softly. She laid a hand on his arm with a butterfly touch. "He has a great deal of sense and knows better than most how to turn a compliment. Yet, not so prettily as some. One does expect a bit more from a man of letters, though."

"Is that a thinly veiled request to hear your loveliness extolled in the words of the poets?" he said with a soft laugh and that faint hint of mockery she had noticed before. "I have always thought the compliment from the heart far surpasses manufactured words of others. But I fear my appreciation for poetry is somewhat limited, and in any case, even those honey words must be tedious to you from repetition."

"Being admired is never tedious," she said, gently scolding. Her sensuous lips pouted slightly. "Perhaps it is I who fail to stimulate you to poetry. Tess no doubt surfeits on your eloquence." She leaned into him a bit, causing the curves of her white breasts, which peeped above the neckline of her thin muslin dress, to be proffered to him like a treat.

"Tessa would smile to hear you say so," he responded mechanically. He was now certain that it was not vanity that made him think she had sought him out deliberately to cast out lures to him. He did not for a moment believe that she wished to embark on a clandestine affair with him and could only suppose that she was determined to add him to her trophies. He was more vexed with himself than with her for this, knowing that he should never have permitted her to suppose he might be smitten with her charms.

He supposed he was well served for his behavior. Now he would have the difficulty of fending off a flirtation with Letitia while at the same time not giving her cause for offense, which he did not doubt would lead to difficulties, for he had noticed the spoiled beauty's spiteful behavior to Tessa. Therefore, he suppressed the desire to tell her flatly that her charms held no interest for him.

A moment's reflection, though, gave him what he thought might be the solution. Unless he entirely misread the character of his sister-in-law, he believed that while Letitia might wish to hear him express his desire for her, she would not at all like to find it displayed.

"Well, Tess is a little prosy, I suppose, to inspire such things," Letitia said without any notion that her words might give offense. "Yet I fancy such words might fall from your lips if you were *truly* stimulated by one you admired."

Jonathan viewed the soft, inviting mouth so close to his own and admitted to himself that his scheme would not at all be a penance to carry out. "Who could be in your company for more than a moment and not be stimulated?" he said lavishly. "It is not only a want of eloquence; you must know I cannot speak."

It was all Letitia could do to keep her sense of triumph from showing in her face. "And I should not be here," she said in tortured accents, "but there are times when the heart does not heed the head."

He placed his hand lightly on her waist and felt her stiffen slightly. "I have been glad that we would leave this house, that I might no longer be tortured to have you so near and so unattainable." He allowed huskiness to slip into his voice. "But if you feel as I do, then I need no longer suffer. We must be discreet, of course; we would not wish to unnecessarily wound Tessa or Walter, and decency must insist that we wait for consummation until after your wedding. But, oh, my love, what delights we shall know until then. I think I can persuade Tessa to postpone our remove until Monday."

He had enough of his mother in him to rather enjoy indulging in these absurdities. It was not easy for him to bite back his own smile of triumph as Letitia nearly gasped in astonishment at his words. "I have shocked you," he said wretchedly. "You must forgive me, fairest one, but to know that you want me as much as I do you is too much for me to contain myself."

Letitia had participated in decorous lovemaking many times—unbeknownst to her betrothed—with a number of young men all of whose tentative embraces she had handled with great ease. Jonathan was the first to openly suggest that he would want more from her than a few stolen kisses, which made her a little nervous of his embrace but not yet concerned. "If only we *might* abandon ourselves to our wishes," she responded, but without her former assurance, "but we must be brave and allow our virtue to ennoble us. Walter apart, every feeling must revolt at so betraying my own sister."

"We could not be condemned for following the insistence of our natures," he said grandly, and sweeping her tight against him, he choked off her startled gasp by placing his lips on hers and kissing her more soundly than she had ever been kissed before.

As soon as she could, she broke away from him and took a stumbling step backward, but he brought her to him again. "My ardour is new and frightening to you," he said deep in his throat, "but you shall see, after the first time that we have lain together . . ."

"I could not!" Letitia managed to gasp. She was rapidly becoming genuinely frightened of the situation, not just because of his ardour, but because she felt as if her own wits had deserted her and she had no idea now how to retrieve this situation. She had after all made up to him, and she wished to save face in this and yet had no intention of abandoning her virtue to him.

"It is only a maiden's fear," he said into her shell-like ear, and kissed her again, crushing her against him in the time-honored display of passion.

Genuinely frightened now, Letitia cared nothing for saving face and only hoped it would not be necessary for her to scream the house down to save her maidenhood. She began to struggle with him in earnest, and he released her a little to regard her. "I have been precipitate?" he asked unhappily. "Or perhaps it is that obstacle which your fine sensibilities cannot overcome. There need be no difficulty. If I know that I can make you mine, no risk is too great. Do you know, my love, if Tessa is ever in the habit of taking laudanum to make her sleep?" These last words were so outrageous that he was certain they must tip his hand, but Letitia's eyes grew round with terror.

"Let me go!" she demanded, her voice hoarse with emotion. "I shall scream if you do not." He did not release her at once, and she made good her promise and gave a strangled cry which was the best she could do under the force of her emotions. It was scarcely enough to bring the house down upon them, but it did penetrate to the front hall nearby. This was totally empty but for Tessa, who had just come in and was standing by the table that held that day's visiting cards. Tessa was not alarmed, but she was curious. She put down the card that she held and went to the bookroom, where she thought the sound had come from.

The sight which greeted her when she opened the door made her feel as if she had been struck with an anvil. Letitia, who was facing the door, saw her come in and gasped out her name, causing Jonathan to release her at last. He turned to face his wife, and Tessa would have been most gratified to know that none of the horror or pain that she felt was visible in the blank expression she presented.

This situation was exactly what Letitia would have wished for and could never have managed to set up, but now that Tessa was actually witness to her husband's betrayal, she was far too upset to play upon it. She felt foolish, chagrined, and frightened and only wanted to be away from the grasp of this libertine. Murmuring a few disjointed phrases, she quitted the room almost at an undignifed run.

Tessa held Jonathan's eyes for a long moment and then turned to follow her sister out of the room without saying a word.

"Tessa!" he called after her, and when she ignored him, he crossed the room in a few quick strides and caught at her arm just as she entered the hall.

Calling every resource she possessed to the fore, she faced him with no more emotion than a cold stare might convey. "This matter speaks for itself, Jon," she said in measured accents. "I see no point in compounding it's tawdriness with excuses or lies, if that is what you intend."

"I intend to explain to you what I was about. Do you really believe that I would be fool enough to seduce your sister in her father's house and beneath your nose?"

Tessa gave him a frigid smile. "Why not? This being my father's house did not prevent you from lovemaking with me, though I suppose you had more motive in that than mere pleasure. Letitia should be flattered, for there is nothing more you could want of her than her person."

"What the devil does that mean?" he asked, his own tone growing icy.

"I think you understand me," she said with a faint sneer. "But don't think I am complaining. On the whole it is a fair enough bargain; being a marchioness is nothing to disdain, particularly for one who is still so close in lineage to the cow byres. I will say that I don't care for my own sister to be a part of your amusements, but you may be reassured that generally I am not dissatisfied with what I have purchased."

Their intimacy was enough now that she knew he would find these words brutally wounding, and speaking from her own pain, it was precisely what she wished. He was thin-lipped and grim-faced and she knew her shafts had gone home.

"I see," he said, his voice steely and clipped. "I must be grateful. Used merchandise is not usually so highly regarded."

"That *is* true," she agreed with a small cool, insulting smile. His eyes blazed so furiously at this that for a moment she feared he would strike her.

"You are most generous, dear wife," he said with elaborate irony. "I see I must only have a care to the sources of my depravity to avoid your censure. It intrigues me though to wonder what it would take to ruffle my cool and lovely mate."

"Perhaps the first time I am unwell after drinking my soup would answer," she replied nastily.

He was startled out of his composure by these words, looking completely thunderstruck. Tessa knew that in referring to poison, however sarcastically, she had gone too far, but she was too upset herself to care. His hand dropped away from her arm and she turned and left him, walking briskly to the stairs and going at once to her bedchamber. Mary was there putting the last of her things in a portmanteau to be taken to Upper Mount Street. She dismissed the girl and stood staring dumbly at the portmanteau. How excited and happy she had been just a few short minutes ago to think that that very night would see them in their own house, truly beginning their married life together. She sat down at her dressing table, leaning on the table and burying her face in her hands.

She was so upset that she felt nearly sick, and for a time she simply sat very still until the shaking inside of her subsided. Her eyes stung with tears, but she did not weep. She did not know the details of what had occurred in the bookroom and she did not wish to know. Whatever her husband's culpability, she did not for a moment doubt that her sister shared in the blame. It would be a prize indeed to Letitia to have added Jonathan to those who sat at her feet, and just the sort of thing she would do to assure herself of her superiority over her sister. Tessa understood her sister too well to hate her for casting out lures to Jonathan, but she was human enough to be grimly satisfied that Jonathan had responded in such a way that Letitia was made to see that she had taken on more than she could handle.

But Tessa did not really care a rush for what Letitia had done or how she had been served. All that occupied her thoughts and emotions was that Jonathan *had* responded to Letitia. With a small bark of ironic laughter, she wondered why she should be so surprised and hurt. Jonathan had never pretended to feeling more for her than friendship and physical attraction, and she doubted that this was enough for most men to pledge their fidelity on. She had even rather respected him for his honesty in not offering her cream pot love, though this respect must be at the cost to her own feelings. Letitia, she was sure, was delight enough to tempt any man, even one who must risk a deal to pursue her.

If her anger was fully vented at anyone it was at herself. How like some stupid plot it was in a wretched melodrama! The cool, self-controlled heiress who is too practical to succumb to the lures of romance meets and falls willy-nilly in love with the handsome fortune hunter who is clever enough to pierce her defenses.

In her first season a friend of hers who was now married and begun on her family had confided to

her that trying to decide which of two suitors for her
hand she could love best was tearing her to pieces.
"You are so fortunate, Tess," she said, "not to be
troubled with delicate sensibilities in these matters.
You will never know what it is to suffer the pangs of
the heart." The words had been sincerely spoken,
but she had admonished her friend, saying that she
considered a want of such fine feelings something of
a misfortune, "for if I don't know the pains of love,
neither do I know its joys." Now she had tasted at
least some of the rapture and she felt that it was not
a fair exchange for the ache, which was infinitely
more acute.

There was a small scratching sound at her door.
Tessa ignored it, but in a few moments Letitia came
into her room uninvited. Tessa regarded her sister
balefully as she approached. "I have the headache,
Letty," she said coldly. "I have no wish or intention
of talking with you."

"You are upset, and how could you be blamed!"
Letitia said unhappily. "Please do not hate me, Tess.
I swear I never meant any harm to you."

"You might have thought of that before you began
making up to my husband," Tessa said plainly, not
in the least concerned with sparing her sister's
feelings.

"I did not make up to him," Letitia began, sounding ill-used, but remembering the purpose of her
visit softened her tone. "At least, I admit I did flirt
with him a bit, but that does not signify, for I *always*
flirt and I mean nothing by it."

"Then if I took the situation correctly," Tessa
replied, "you have learned that it can be a dangerous thing to do."

"Oh, yes," Letitia said breathily. "Tess, I am so
sorry for you. I had no idea he was such a loose fish.
Thank heaven you came in when you did, for I am
certain he meant to ravish me then and there."

"In a house filled with servants?" Tessa asked

disdainfully. "I shouldn't think so. And you may save your pity. Hartfield is not a loose fish, whatever you may think, and I have no intention of falling into hysteria and casting him from my life, though I don't doubt that would give you the satisfaction you wished when you began casting out the lures to him in the first place."

Letitia uttered a tiny resentful gasp at this attack. She had assured herself that her motive in coming to her sister was to warn her what manner of man she had married before she found herself sharing a fate similar to that of Constance. The fact that Tessa might justly accuse her of far worse than she had was forgotten or simply ignored. "What a perfectly *horrid* thing to say! *You* would be served if I were to leave at once without warning you, which is what I have come to do despite the embarrassment of the unhappy scene you discovered me in."

Tessa sighed, deciding that further argument would likely prolong Letitia's stay. That young woman was never averse to the drama of a heated exchange. "What am I in danger of, Letty? Discovering that my husband has the wanderlust of a cat? That is no greater a revelation than is made to most wives. You may well learn it yourself one day."

Letitia ignored this slur against Torrance's adoration of her. "Tess," she said, lowering her voice dramatically, "he is a dangerous man. It would not be wise in me to speak too much, but please take care of yourself when you are in Upper Mount Street. Do not trust him more than you must. Think of poor Constance and be careful."

Tessa blinked at her, uncertain that she could be understanding Letitia properly. "Are you suggesting that I avoid sleeping draughts?" she asked incredulously, and then completely disconcerted and annoyed her sister by bursting into laughter.

"There is nothing to laugh about. *Constance* is no longer laughing."

"Don't be absurd, Letty," she advised scornfully.

"If you find yourself killed for your fortune, you will not think me so absurd."

"If I find myself killed for any reason, I don't suppose I shall be able to think anything at all," Tessa said with maddening practicality.

"You know what I mean."

"Yes. And I also know that Jonathan did not profit at all from Constance's death. You should know yourself that it was very much the reverse."

"If you do not wish to be warned and listen to reason, then there is no point in talking to you." Letitia answered with a pout, and turning on her heel, flounced out of the room.

Tessa sighed again. There was nothing for it but to put on her best face and go on. She certainly had no intention of allowing her marriage to Jonathan to deteriorate to the mess that he had had with Constance. She was hardly the first woman to find herself in love with a man who felt little more than liking for her. Often she had heard herself described as self-possessed and unemotional, and that was exactly the mask she would don now. No one, particularly not Jonathan, would ever know that she felt as if a part of her life had ended when she had opened the door to the library.

Tessa rose and rang for her maid to finish the packing, then said and did all that was necessary before the servants and family. At last she and Jonathan entered the carriage and were driven to Upper Mount Street. It was a journey of painful silence that neither cared to break. Dinner was more bearable only because she sat down to it alone, he having sent word to the kitchen that he would be dining that night at Watier's. This was sadly different from the first meal in their new home that she had imagined.

Tessa passed a restless, unhappy night and awoke the next morning with a genuine headache. She toyed with the idea of taking a breakfast tray in her room, but decided that this was craven. If putting a good face on things was what she meant to do, it was as well to begin doing so at once.

In most of the romances that Tessa had read, when the heroine was dealt a blow to the heart, she was usually so completely devastated that she was unable to function normally, and instead would cancel all of her activities to brood wretchedly by staring out of panes that always seemed to be rain-soaked. This leisure was seldom granted to women in the real world.

She dressed plainly for a day she meant to spend absorbed in housekeeping chores and went downstairs. Jonathan greeted her with what she thought was a hint of anxiousness in his eyes when she entered the breakfast room, and she was not really surprised when he insisted on speaking with her privately after they had finished their meal.

Tessa did not at all wish to hear his excuses, but she knew that if they were to go on with any semblance of normalcy, she would have to do so eventually, and she quietly agreed. She gave him her complete attention as he explained himself. He told her most plainly that he had formed the habit of flirting with Letitia for his own reprehensible amusement. Gallantly giving Letitia as little of the blame as possible, he told her the complete truth of the encounter in the bookroom and finished by apologizing for taking umbrage at her anger and compounding the matter with anger of his own. The only thing he did not mention was her implication that he had married her principally for her fortune and that she had wanted to gain enoblement from his title. That was a topic that Tessa knew must be too sensitive between them, and she was glad to be spared its revival.

She heard him out and at the end calmly accepted his story. "I am forever telling Letty that she is overly dramatic, but I did behave rather like a trage-dienne myself yesterday," she admitted handsomely, and coming as near as she dared to the forbidden topic, added, "I said dreadful things, too. I hope *you* will forgive me, Jon, and not think that I mean to enact Cheltenham tragedies for you whenever my imagination runs away with me."

He regarded her calm, unconcerned visage for a long moment and then said, "No, I know you would not. There is nothing for *me* to forgive. If you will just believe that I meant nothing toward your sister, I hope we may be comfortable with each other again."

"Of course we may!" she said with a smile that did not reach her eyes. Her feelings were still too raw, though, to be restrained indefinitely, and she stood abruptly, and added, "I must ask you to ex-cuse me now, the housekeeper and cook are both waiting for me and must be thinking me a most capricious mistress. There is so much to be seen to until we are completely settled in that I can only hope you have entertainments enough to keep you occupied. I fear you will find yourself sadly ne-glected by your wife."

"I think I can contrive to amuse myself," he said with one of those quick smiles that nearly threw her into confusion. Murmuring something about menus, she lowered her eyes from his and left the room. Jonathan sat down again slowly, and stared pen-sively at the pattern in the carpet for the better part of the next hour.

This was hardly the sort of thing he had had in mind when he had spoken of self-amusement, but he was very far from bored. What he thought of as he sat was his first marriage. He compared it with his second, and the conclusions he drew chilled him.

Chapter Eight

The first sennight of settling in and becoming used to an entirely new establishment ate up time and troubles for both Lord and Lady Hartfield. Their breakfast, luncheon, and dinner conversation was perfectly felicitous at all times. There was never again a mention of the incident with Letitia, nor of the motives of either for marrying the other. For all the world to see, they were a content, even a happy pair.

But the warmth was gone. Tessa noted it, deplored it, and wondered which of them was to blame. At times she was certain that it was his fault, that in fact there never had been any warm feeling between them beyond the heat of passion and whatever fantasies she had had to embellish the truth. At other times she was equally convinced that it was her own wariness of him and the close guard she kept on her feelings that had doused whatever sparks had existed between them.

Whatever the cause, Tessa felt completely powerless to change the state of things. If Jonathan could not feel more than friendship for her, she did not know what she could do to change him. The shafts of pain she had known that day she had found him with Letitia must make her cautious about ever giving herself to him as completely as once she had done.

It was not Tessa's nature to dwell on her own wretchedness, particularly when she did not know the solution to it. The best thing—in fact, the only thing—she knew to do was to put it out of her mind as much as she could and go on with her life. It helped to remind herself that it was seldom the big joys or hurts in life that could throw one into complete confusion, but the disruption of the commonplaces. So she set about the task of applying her energies to making their hired house into a true, comfortable home. A man may have his passions, her mother had once told her, but when all was said and done, it was his comforts that mattered to him the most.

The servants they had hired to staff the house were to a man unexceptionable, and Tessa knew that once the confusion had settled, the house would virtually run by itself. Then her restless energies would have to find another outlet. After casting about for a scheme to apply them to, she decided that she could do worse than see to her own embellishment. Colin's idea that she should take on a very distinct and dashing style exactly appealed to her at this time, largely, she supposed, because her vanity was exactly now in need of a boost.

She had an idea of how she wished to proceed, but she decided to consult carefully with Colin, not only to discover what he had had in mind and to gain an opinion more objective than her own, but because Colin's taste in all matters of ton was seldom faulted. If he said a thing would take, it did; what he declared was not at all the thing seldom was.

Colin was delighted to be of service. He carefully scheduled his duties to be sure of some time each day to spend on the project, for, he said to his cousin, "No point in doing the thing at all if it's going to be halfway. We'll put you together properly and you'll make your come-out, so to speak. It wouldn't do at all to have 'em raising their quizzing glasses at you one night and stumbling over your name the next."

Tessa agreed and begged pardon for not being aware that she was now such a nonentity. The amenities settled and the plan of action drawn, they began to carry it out on the Friday that marked the sennight since the move to Upper Mount Street. The following week was marked by feverish activity for Tessa. Her housekeeping chores completed, morning calls paid or received, she barely found time to snatch a light luncheon before Colin called for them to begin on their shopping expeditions.

"If I had guessed how much time I would spend being held together with pins," she complained one afternoon late in the week, "I think I might have preferred remaining anonymous."

They were in Madame Celeste's, a most exclusive and expensive modiste who catered to the needs of ladies of rank and fashion. They were in one of the small private parlours where friends were allowed to view creations, and she was pirouetting before the multiple mirrors at the far end of the room. Colin critically surveyed the lavender walking dress and after informing the seamstress of the way he would wish to see the sleeves cut, he nodded his approval. "You won't be saying that the first time you walk into an assembly and every head turns to you instead of Letty." He told the needle woman that they would now be ready to try the cherry-red ball gown that Madame had spoken of.

Tessa protested at the prospect of being basted into any more gowns, and declared that she did not think cherry red her color.

"Nonsense," said Colin perfunctorily. "You are just afraid of it. The word 'dashing' and the name of

Lady Hartfield won't be synonymous if you are craven."

"They are more likely to use the term 'high-flier,'" Tessa said caustically a bit later as she viewed herself in the cherry-red ball gown that was as daring in cut as in color. "I shall look a perfect quiz in this, Colin. I'll stand out like a beacon."

"Exactly," he said behind her.

Tessa continued to protest for several more minutes, but in the end was made to see that the gown flattered her figure and brought out her coloring in a rather magnificent way. Actually she vetoed only a very few of his choices, and then more to remain in command of the situation than because she mistrusted his taste or judgment.

As they were about to leave the shop, Madame Celeste herself came to Tessa to compliment her on her taste and the God-given gifts that permitted her to dress with flair, and to tell her that one of my lady's purchases from earlier in the week was ready to be sent to her house, unless Tessa should care to take it with her. Tessa was about to have it sent home, but Colin insisted not only that they take the dress but also that Tessa return to the changing room and put it on for his inspection.

It was another walking dress, this time in emerald green and again of a bold and flattering cut. Standing once again before the mirrors, Tessa was forced to admit that it became her beyond her expectations. When she saw this dress, the first example of her new style, her last doubts about the scheme were reconciled. Colin suggested that she wear the dress home to try out the effect, and she agreed, secretly wondering if she would run into Jonathan, and what he would think.

The effect was seen at once and was most gratifying when, as they walked a little more down the street to the milliner's, they met up with two acquaintances of her husband. These gentlemen, who before had been correctly kind and courteous toward her, now greeted her with open admiration. When they had passed, Tessa accused Colin of having engineered the meeting, but he laughed and denied it, clearly pleased to take the compliment to himself as her mentor.

He accepted her offer to come in for a glass of Madeira when they returned to Upper Mount Street, and they sat in one of the comfortable first-floor saloons discussing their plan and their day. He declined her offer of dinner, pleading a prior engagement, and at last admitted that he had ecclesiastical matters waiting to occupy him.

"I am glad that you have decided to trust me," he said as he rose. "Or perhaps I should say trust yourself. I give you my word, Tess, Letty will look nearly commonplace beside you, and by the time you and Hartfield leave for Boxwood, he'll be dashed glad to be getting you away from the legion of your admirers."

Tessa laughed at his nonsense, but felt a wistful urge that the last at least might come true. Jonathan came into the room at about that moment to find Colin and Tessa standing close, sharing a private amusement. Tessa was wearing a dress he could not recall seeing before but which he thought suited her better than any other he had ever known her to wear. She looked particularly fine, her features alight with pleasure, her McAffe blood much in evidence, causing her and Colin to present a picture that was most charming and attractive but which Jonathan did not view with any particular enjoyment. He greeted McAffe amiably, wished most insincerely that Colin might extend his stay, and when he had gone, sat down in the chair McAffe had vacated. Tessa sat down again as well, and began to gather together their glasses and plates.

"Leave it," he said shortly. "The servants will clear it."

Tessa looked up at the unexpected sharpness in his tone. "I know, but there is no need to leave a mess."

"Servants expect a mistress who knows her place as well as they know theirs," he said in a tone that was plainly argumentative.

Tessa had no idea what his ill-humor was about, but since she could think of no cause in anything she had done, she assumed it was just a foul mood that had overtaken him and had no intention of being drawn into an argument not of her choosing. But neither did she mean to bow to his tempers. She nodded coolly in acknowledgment of his implied criticism and calmly ignored him by continuing with her task.

"You have been spending rather a lot of time with McAffe of late," he said leadingly.

She looked up and favored him with a chilly smile. "Are you going to suggest what people might say?" she asked. Believing him indifferent to her, she did not suppose that he was accusing her of playing him false; she did not believe he would care, any more than he had with Constance; but was sure he might care a great deal if talk of her were to begin. She knew that he had hated the disgrace Constance had brought to his name. "There is nothing to concern you. Colin and I have been going about together since our nursery days. No one pays it the least mind."

"I understood he was employed. The archbishop must be a lenient man."

"I expect Colin only had to inform him that he would be spending his time helping me with some matters and the thing was accomplished," said Tessa. "Papa's grandfather, the one who was raised on a farm in Shropshire, rose to be the Bishop of Exeter, you know, and was influential in helping the archbishop's career. He is a generous man and has not forgotten."

"Is that how your cousin obtained his position?" Jonathan asked, and Tessa thought there was a hint of nastiness in his tone.

A little extra coolness slipped into her own. "I believe my Uncle Stephen arranged it for him when Colin said he would prefer a staff position to a living of his own. *Some* consideration may have been given to Colin's connexion with this family. I wouldn't know."

"Connexion and preferment are often synonymous terms."

Tessa did not wish for an argument, but neither did she care to hear her cousin and dearest friend maligned, even by her husband. "Colin is an intelligent, capable man," she said stoutly. "If he obtained advancement through patronage, he has done honor to his position through his work and dedication, so to suggest that he receives preferential treatment is unjust."

"It was you who first suggested that he had mentioned your name," Jonathan pointed out. "But if he has such a surfeit of talent and ability, no doubt it was unnecessary, as is your defense of him."

"He is my cousin and my friend," Tessa said sharply. "Of course I shall defend him against scurrilous attack. I am sure you would not have me do less by you. In fact, you surprise me, Jonathan. I had thought that you liked Colin."

"I find him well enough," Jonathan replied shortly. "But it is your choice of him as a friend and confidant that is at question."

"*Is* that what is at question?" Tessa said, pushing the small table the refreshments had been on aside and standing. "I think that it is *you* who are questioning my right to choose my own friends. I may not wonder at it, given your experience with Constance, but you shall have to take my word for it that I shall not disgrace you in my choices as she did. I do not intend to allow anyone to dictate to me whom I should see and whom I should not."

He had succeeded in goading her into as bad a temper as his own, but she still did not mean to involve herself in a verbal battle with him and risk unguarding her tongue in the heat of the moment. In a grand gesture, made more effective by the elegance of her mode, she swept magnificently past him and out of the room to end the unprofitable discussion.

Jonathan remained in the room and poured some of the wine they had left for himself. He cursed himself for a fool, but he could not help the feelings that had caused him to lash out at her. The spectre of Constance, or rather his wretched marriage to her, rose before him. To give oneself to another only to find the gift scorned might happen to anyone; he indulged in no self-pity for the wound that had been dealt to him by his first wife. Nor was he of a disposition that would cause him ever to shy away from love because of one bad experience. But there were so many similarities between this marriage and his first, that he could not prevent his wariness or fears.

His nastiness to Tessa was a response typical of one he might have made to Constance in a similar situation, but Tessa had done nothing to warrant his severity, and even if he did begin to feel that he would be wise to be watchful of her with Colin, it would not do for him to make more of the thing than it deserved. His suspicions did not blind him to the fact that giving them vent might well jeopardize his own relationship with Tessa. The guard he kept on his feelings, he knew, would have to extend to his tongue as well if what harmony was left to them was to continue.

Tessa went up to her room to change, still angry with him, but this cooled fairly rapidly. She *did* understand that his attack was defensiveness, but that he should think that tongues would start wagging about her and Colin was completely absurd. So absurd that even through her anger she was amused. Still, she did not like to think that Jonathan meant to make a habit of questioning her behavior in such a way. That would have been intolerable. It was yet another difficulty in their relationship that would have to be gotten through, but she had not been feeling entirely the thing since she had first come home, and her condition was rapidly worsening.

As soon as she was undressed, she deemed it prudent to lie down on her bed in a darkened room. She was not alarmed by her sudden headache or the unpleasant waves of nausea; she had so far escaped most of the less pleasurable aspects of pregnancy that most women were prey to, and merely supposed that her time had come at last.

She closed her eyes, breathed deeply, and forced her thoughts away from all unpleasantness, supposing that the tensions of her problems would hardly be beneficial to her distress. She was reasonably successful at this and in a short while drifted into a light sleep.

When she opened her eyes again, she saw Jonathan standing next to the post at the bottom of her bed. "Mary told me you were feeling unwell and resting," he said softly. "She disapproved of me for wishing to bother you, I think, but I wished to apologize to you for the things that I said before. My humor was foul and I vented it on you."

Tessa had not expected this, but was feeling too poorly to find any enthusiasm for his handsome apology. "It doesn't signify," was all that she said in a lackluster tone.

He gazed down at her for a very long moment and then left her without saying anything else. Tessa sighed, supposing that he had misunderstood and would now be angry again. It was yet another hurdle to be gotten over, but she could not think of that now. She closed her eyes, hoping to again fall into sleep.

A short time later she again opened her eyes and saw Jonathan coming back into the room. He was carrying a glass of greenish-white liquid and he came directly to her and sat beside her on the edge of the bed.

"Sit up and drink this," he ordered. "It will make you feel much more the thing."

"What is it?" Tessa asked suspiciously. She did not at all wish to sit up and upset what she felt was a delicate balance, and the liquid in the glass looked exactly the sort of evil concoction that one's nurse used to force upon one in the nursery.

"It's a recipe of my mother's. She regards it as a panacea and particularly recommends it for breeding sicknesses."

"But what is in it?" Tessa demanded, and there was no mistaking the dubiousness in her voice.

"Not a drop of laudanum," he said dryly.

Tessa could not misunderstand him, and even feeling as wretched as she did, she could not allow *this* misunderstanding to come between them. "I did not mean that," she said carefully.

"Didn't you?" he said coolly. "It is principally milk with several common kitchen herbs crushed and blended together. I did not even make it with my own hands, but gave the recipe to Cook, so you may drink it with relative unconcern."

"You are willfully misunderstanding me," she said dully, "and I am feeling far too horrid to find any help for it. Please just give me the thing if you think it will help."

"Are you certain?"

"Yes."

He handed her the glass and she drank it, discovering that it was not nearly so bad-tasting as it looked. She gave him back the glass and lay down again and closed her eyes.

He left her at once, more upset now than he had been after their quarrel. Even if she did not mean to imply that he would wish to give her something harmful in the cordial, he knew that at the least the thought had been in her mind. He recalled a similar remark she had made the day she had found him in her father's bookroom with Letitia.

He knew that she had said it only to hurt him, but the fact that Tessa, whom he had always regarded as the one person who completely believed in him, could even in a moment of anger doubt his innocence added yet one more layer to the wall that seemed to be inexorably building between them.

Tessa did not know whether his defensiveness was still the result of his foul mood or whether he really believed that she thought him guilty of murdering Constance and having similar designs against her. That he could believe any such thing seemed absurd in light of her behavior toward him from the very beginning, but given the misunderstandings that cropped up between them so much of late, she supposed it was not impossible. Her next thought was to some extent induced by her sickness, but it took unhappy hold in her mind. She wondered if they were headed down a road similar to the one he had trodden with Constance, if they could find happiness at even the level of friendship, and worst of all, if there was any point in trying.

Tessa did not fall asleep again, and within an hour or so felt so much better that she got out of bed and later consented to take a light dinner tray in her room. However, she was not feeling so completely cured that she cared to go down for her dinner, especially because she did not wish for the encounter with her husband.

By the next morning she was feeling as well as she ever had, and whether this was due to the dowager's brew or would have occurred of its own accord, she could not say. She thanked Jonathan for the drink he had had made up for her, but felt constrained from mentioning the misunderstanding that had come about with it.

As the days passed, they were still getting on very well together on the surface, and practically, little had changed in their behavior toward each other, but anything approaching intimacy was becoming increasingly strained between them. As long as they were in company or even alone with servants about, their amiability toward one another was complete, but the moment they were forced to deal exclusively with one another, a tension arose between them that was nearly a tangible thing. Inevitably their lovemaking became first nearly impersonal and then ceased completely.

This more than anything made Tessa unhappy, for their physical intimacy was the closest thing to an expression of love as existed between them, and the loss of it, she feared, meant the eventual loss of all intimacy. Certainly it appeared as if that course were already set. She wanted to talk with him about it, but her tongue, usually so free, seemed to be tied in knots the moment she attempted to broach the subject.

Tessa was spending much of her free time now with her mother and sister, helping with all the minute and tiresome details of arranging Letitia's wedding and the following wedding breakfast. Letitia had been a bit cool toward Tessa for several days after the incident in the bookroom, but the relations between the sisters had settled at least into the amiable rivalry that was common to them. They never once spoke of that day, and Jonathan was never a topic between them.

Letitia had by now had the leisure to think over her encounter with Jonathan and had come to the infuriating conclusion that his behavior had been deliberately outrageous. It did not occur to her that it might have been a counter to her own less-than-admirable behavior, but she thought that his purpose was self-amusement. She now perceived that his laughing mockery was at her expense and her brother-in-law was as deep in her black looks as it was possible for an attractive man who had paid her some attention to be. And rather than suppose that he might not be attracted to her beauty, she assumed that Tessa had in some way maligned her to him and his derision was the result. And the result of these thoughts of hers was that she was determined in some way to pay both back. She was too occupied with her approaching nuptials to concoct a new scheme, but she had patience.

Tessa was happily unaware of her sister's pettiness and plotting; she had more than enough to occupy her mind and would have dreaded yet another difficulty.

The lionization of her and Jonathan as a couple had settled down after their first month back in the world, but their calendar was filled until the very day of Letitia's wedding. All the bustle of entertainment combined with the preparation for the wedding made intimacy difficult in any event, and Tessa told herself that she would deal with the matter when they were at last retired to Boxwood. For the present she was always civil to him and never out of sorts, and in return he was equally pleasant, never again subjecting her to his ill-tempers.

Tessa's excursions with Colin became fewer, not because of anything that Jonathan had said to her that day, but because there was less need for them. She had more dresses and gowns now, she declared, than the princess royal. After the green walking dress, most of the other gowns ordered had begun to arrive and Tessa's new style was put into effect at once. The results were as dramatic as the reception she had met with in the street from Jonathan's acquaintances, and while the gentlemen admired, the women envied. By the end of a sennight, Tessa became aware that she was being paid the great compliment of being copied. So used was she to being overshadowed by Letitia that this was heady wine for her, and she basked in the attentiveness of her new court with great delight.

The only blight to her pleasure in this was Jonathan's reaction. She had followed Colin's scheme, not from a wish to outshine Letitia or to make herself attractive to other men, but to regain her flagging self-confidence and to heighten the interest of the one man that mattered to her, her husband. Instead it seemed to her that he resented her new style, and it only caused constraint between them.

For a bit she wondered if he might be feeling jealousy or possessiveness, but she was forced to admit that this was just her own fancy. He would not again care to suffer the world branding him as a cuckold, and for this reason he would countenance no indiscretion on her part with Colin. As long as she did not make a scandal, though, she did not suppose he would care how many men might flock to her side. It was not even as if he were deposed, for they were hardly in the habit of living unfashionably in one another's pocket.

Their circumstances would soon be changing in any event. It wanted little more than a fortnight to Letitia's wedding now, and already the season was beginning to wind down a bit as a family or two who did not consider viewing Letitia taking her vows with Lord Torrance a "not-to-be-missed" event, left the city to pursue pleasures more suited to the coming warm months.

It was at about this time that Tessa actually found herself with a day with little to occupy her socially except a dinner invitation that did not particularly appeal to her. Jonathan, she knew, was engaged for the evening with a number of friends who intended to take their revels to the Daffy Club and Cribb's

Parlour, and she doubted he would return home before the early hours of the morning.

On impulse she canceled her engagement and ordered dinner from her own kitchen, deciding to spend the day caring for some chores that needed attending to before the packing for the remove to Boxwood began, and the evening simply resting and perhaps at last devoting thought to her marriage and the sorry state it was now in.

This first was accomplished smoothly, and dinner was more gotten out of the way than enjoyed. She had changed for dinner, partly out of habit, partly to keep her spirits up. She retired to the smaller drawing room, the proportions of which were more suited for a quiet lonely evening than the formal drawing room or any of the saloons. Before she could apply her mind to her cogitations, Colin called with a message for her from his mother, and she persuaded him to remain for a few minutes to take a bit of wine with her.

She then turned her reluctant thoughts toward her husband, herself, and their marriage. It seemed to her that she rehashed every minute detail of their relationship a half-dozen times, with no more inkling of how they were to go on than she had had before she had begun.

She was curled into a corner of a sofa, so deep in thought that she barely noticed the clock on the mantel striking the hour of eleven and did not at all hear Jonathan when he came into the room. He spoke her name, and she was so startled that she sat up and gaped at him, warmth flooding into her cheeks.

Jonathan's eyes narrowed as he regarded her, but his voice was amiable enough when he spoke. "Are you feeling well?" he asked, coming up to her and sitting beside her. "I thought you were promised to the Endicotts this evening." He saw her eyes avoid his and involuntarily tensed his muscles. It was a sensation with which he was not unfamiliar, but which he had not felt since the night of his discovery of Constance and Sir Richard in the anteroom of the Bellamy house, and one which he had hoped never to feel again.

"Why should I not be well?" Tessa responded a bit haltingly. "You are thinking of the afternoon that I was taken ill, but I assure you that since then I have been most hale. I have not told Mamma yet of my condition, but I shall before we leave for Boxwood, and I know she will marvel at my health, for she has said a thousand times how she suffered with Letty and me."

This was chatter to cover her confusion, and he was not deceived by it. "I am a little surprised to find you alone. The footman who let me in told me you had a visitor," he said blandly.

Tessa knit her brow for a moment. "Oh! I collect he means Colin, but that was nearly two hours ago."

"Perhaps it was not noticed when he left."

"Perhaps," Tessa agreed uncomfortably. She wished that he had chosen one of the chairs across from her, for she found his nearness disconcerting. It was not just that his return had been unexpected and had startled her. Her thoughts had been so intimately wrapped in him at the moment that she feared her heart must show clearly on her sleeve, and this her pride forbade.

"I seem to be discomfiting you," he said quietly, as if reading her mind, and succeeded in increasing her confusion to the point that she felt like an idiot schoolgirl.

Taking herself firmly in hand, she answered with better control in her voice. "I should have said 'startled.' I didn't think to see you before breakfast."

"*Think* to see or *hope* to see," he said abruptly. "I won't subject us to the farce of shaking out the curtains or peering beneath the furniture to see if

McAffe is to be discovered, but I think I have warned you not to assume me complaisant."

This sudden attack of his was not only disconcerting and confusing but also all the more stinging for its unexpectedness. "Do you suppose I have stuffed my cousin up the chimney to hide him?" was her angry rejoinder. "You may search if you choose, or perhaps you would simply prefer to adopt the civilized approach and discreetly retire until he can brush the soot from his breeches and make good his escape. You must take the lead in this, for you've no doubt had practice in these matters."

"You need no lead from me in the matter of carrying off clandestine meetings," he said nastily.

Her lips parted in surprise at his deliberately offensive tone. She had not meant for this to escalate into another quarrel between them, but the unflinching challenge in his eyes told her plainly that almost anything she might have said would have been kindling enough, and his injustice, particularly in light of how she had actually spent her evening, was enough to set off an answering spark in her. "And I shall not presume to instruct you in the proper conduct of a discreet cuckold," she replied with a viciousness to match his own.

His eyes were hard and angry, his nostrils slightly flared; she thought for a moment that he might strike her, and willed herself not to flinch away from him.

He had no notion to vent his fury in a physical way, but there was violence in his emotions. Once again the wounds to his pride and heart were open, once again he was giving rein to his suspicions, and once again he could help neither how he felt nor what he said. Intellectually he knew these things, but it was not his intellect that ruled him now. "I see that Constance gave you enough of her company for you to take her for the model of a harridan, or is it that the role comes naturally for women with more money than moral principles?"

"Perhaps it is just the natural conduct of any woman unfortunate enough to find herself your wife?" she said with no thought to what her words might produce. The effect was visible at once. His eyes narrowed almost to slits as his heavy lids hid their expression completely, and his mouth tightened to an unyielding line, but she was every bit as upset as he now and didn't care or fear him. "How dare you speak in such a way to me?" she asked, her anger almost making her voice a hiss.

"How dare *you* throw McAffe in my face in my own house? Do you suppose I haven't seen you pandering to his opinions, deferring to his taste even in the matter of your own dress?" His tone was crisp and biting. "I will grant you the fashion of setting up a *cicisbeo*, but I'll have no man setting himself up in my house as your lapdog."

Tears of pure rage stung at her eyes at this ill-usage, but she blinked them back for fear that he would mistake the emotion behind them. "Is that why you left London for Gillane a few years ago? Did Connie's litter of 'lapdogs' get underfoot?" She felt she could not sit beside him for another moment, and she started to rise, but he drew her back by grabbing her wrist in a crushing grasp.

"You know nothing of the circumstances of my marriage to Constance," he said furiously. "You would be wise not to presume with me in any way."

"Nor would you be wise to presume with me," she retorted with equal heat, ignoring the pain of his constricting hold. "I am not Constance," she added, nearly spitting out her words.

"Not yet."

He let go of her wrist and she stood at once. "If this is the sort of nasty, unpredictable manner you took with her, perhaps I can begin to understand her better and not give her so much of the blame.

It goes well beyond presumption for you to judge my character in such a way on so little evidence."

"*You* dislike being judged on little evidence?" he asked sardonically, raising his eyes to hers but remaining seated. "There is nothing you can teach me on that head. Your accusations about Letitia were no better founded, but you chose to see and hear what you wished. When I am unfaithful to you, dear wife, I assure you that my interest will be engaged beyond the wish to teach a spoiled beauty not to play dangerous games." He rose. "To you I am a philandering fortune hunter and there is an end of it. The wonder of it is that I had dared to hope it might be different with you. You are not Connie, but our marriage is shaping into a fair facsimile of that which I had with her. My surprise over it amounts to naiveté. The world has ever suspected my motives, why not you too?"

This last was spoken almost wearily, and Tessa, struck by his words and his admission that his thoughts on their marriage were so near to her own fears, felt the desire for argument seep away from her. "And you do the same to me," she said quietly, hopelessly.

Jonathan held her eyes for a long moment. "Perhaps it is infectious," he said tonelessly. "Like the pox," he added, then left.

Chapter Nine

That night Jonathan's words to his wife bore fruit beyond any expectation of his. Faced with his accusations, both the reasonable and the unreasonable, and frightened by both the violent turn their argument had taken and the flat despair with which it had ended, Tessa took herself in command and made herself look at the situation more carefully than her heart had yet permitted. She feared the complete destruction of their relationship if she did not find some solution to their misunderstandings and mistrust of each other. The fire had died to embers and the candles were near guttering before she at last went up to her room.

She reviewed their relations again, this time with as much objectivity as she could, trying to see how he might have felt in certain instances as well as recalling what her own emotions had been.

Everything, she thought, had been well enough between them until the morning after she had spent the night with him, and that she now saw had marked the change in her own attitude toward him. Before that she had behaved with confidence in their mutual regard for each other, but afterward, when the intimacy had meant that they had surpassed mere friendship, she had become unsure of herself and of him.

Going to him at Newgate and insisting that he marry her had been an act of boldness, but that had been born of desperation, not just for her own unhappy situation but to save him as well. She should have realized it would be inevitable that awkwardness would result from this unusual courtship and marriage, but she, the great unromantic, had nevertheless expected flowery emotions from him when she herself had withdrawn for fear of being wounded. Might not he have felt the same?

The thing with Letitia, if she could believe him—and largely she did—had been blown out of proportion by no one but herself, and the resulting constraint could be traced to no other source. If from there the misunderstandings were his, could she blame him? Hadn't she given him no quarter and made it clear to him that she assumed theirs was a marriage of convenience with no more than a perfunctory liking on both sides?

By the time she at last snuffed out the candles and ascended the stairs, she had made him out a pattern card of virtue and herself heartless and very, very foolish. Even as she thought these things, she realized it was a swing to the other extreme and that the cause and the solution to their problems probably lay with them both. The thing she knew for certain, though, was that this state of affairs could not be allowed to continue even another day. If she continued to behave in this absurd missish way, she believed that between them she and Jonathan would contrive to make their marriage the travesty his had been with Constance.

As she passed the door to his bedchamber, she very nearly went in to awaken him and speak with him at once, but she pushed her eagerness aside for practicality. After breakfast, when they were both rested and her own mind had cleared, would be a

far more sensible time. She did not know whether to
laugh or cry at herself when she realized how little
sense she had shown in the past months. The cool,
in-command woman she was noted to be had been
only a creature of the surface, and Tessa hoped that
she would now be able to meld her self-possession
to her newer, frightening emotions and make herself
the sort of woman she wished herself to be.

Tessa was awake early the next morning despite
her late hours the night before. She washed and
dressed quickly without affecting her new style, in a
simple dress of blue muslin which she knew became
her. She took great pains with the remainder of her
toilette, for she wanted the confidence of knowing
she looked as attractive as possible.

Jonathan was not at table when she entered the
breakfast room, and although this was disappointing,
it was far from dismaying. She ate leisurely, supposing he must soon be down, but when she was done
he still did not appear. It was early enough for her to
doubt that he had been before her, and she went up
to his rooms expecting to find him there. But they
proved as empty as the breakfast room, and, more
daunting, had already seen the hand of a housemaid,
so that it was clear that he had risen betimes.

Tessa could not think where he might be gone at
such an early hour and returned downstairs to search
the library or any other room likely to contain him.
This proved fruitless: It was clear he had gone from
the house. Swallowing her pride, she summoned his
valet and admitted that she had no idea of the whereabouts of her husband by asking if he knew where
his master was to be found.

The valet, seeming more puzzled by her question
than pitying, replied that his lordship had left near
at dawn to attend the prizefight near Cheltenham,
as he'd planned.

All her plans blown to bits by this news, Tess felt

stunned, but had the wits to dismiss the servant with only appropriate comment. She went up to her sitting room as cast down as before she had been in alt. A search of her memory recalled to her that he had mentioned his intention of going to Cheltenham, but she had not known the date and in any event she had completely forgotten it.

She was more vexed by this than upset. She didn't suppose the delay would change anything. It was simply infuriating. The only thing that concerned her was that the level of emotion that she had hoped would help to make her eloquent would as likely as not evaporate in the three days she recalled he had told her he would be away.

But it was stupid to brood over what could not be helped. She had promised to make a call on an elderly maternal great-aunt and she changed again for the street and went about her business for the day.

Tessa met her mother later that afternoon at Gunther's and allowed herself to be cajoled into spending another morning helping Lady Frances with wedding arrangements. Since she had no plans for the following morning and Jonathan would be from home in any event, she pledged herself for the following day.

Tessa had nearly made up her mind to spend another night at home alone, but a lonely, depressing meal was enough to change her mind. She was invited to a small party being given in honor of a distant cousin and had told her mother when they met to tender her excuses to the hostess. Knowing it would look odd in her to now make an appearance anyway, she nevertheless rang for her maid to change.

Lady Frances was one of the first people Tessa met when she entered the main saloon, and that lady was decidedly put out by her daughter's appearance. "I just said you were laid low with the migraine not a half-hour ago. It makes me look like a

liar or senile or worse," she said peevishly, and
Tessa was able to soothe her ruffled feathers only by
promising to make up the seating plan for the wedding breakfast herself.

As usual, people who had been invited to more
than one function spent a portion of their time at
each, so by the time midnight had come and gone, a
large part of the company had changed, though the
rooms thrown open for entertainment were still
comfortably filled. As a family member and because
she had no desire to go anywhere else, Tessa remained
the whole evening. She meant to go from here to her
own bed, hopefully to fall into a pleasantly exhausted
sleep. But her plans were to be foiled and much of
her night was to remain sleepless.

There was not the least notion of this when she
smiled a greeting to Colin, who was one of the latest
arrivals. "I didn't think to see you tonight," she said
as he sat beside her in the supper room.

"Mamma said I must give Cousin Martha a look-in
at the least, or gain her severest displeasure," he
replied in explanation.

"And seeing it is nearly one in the morning, 'at
the least' is exactly what you've done."

Colin gave her a boyishly apologetic smile. "Frankly, I cannot abide Cousin Martha, and her mamma
makes me fidget."

Left to themselves in the corner of the room among
the dowagers and chaperones, they settled in for a
comfortable gossip about family and mutual friends.
Their exclusiveness, as Tessa had told Jonathan,
caused no comment, for it was too commonplace,
but, Tessa reminded herself, Jonathan was jealous of
her friendship with Colin. She might not be willing
to give it up, but at least she need not flaunt it in his
face. Bringing the conversation to a quicker end than
she might otherwise have done, she rose, claiming a
wish to speak to her mother before she left.

"Yes," said Colin, "but before you go, there's

something I should tell you. I've been putting it off because it isn't very pleasant, but I think you should know."

Tessa sighed. The last thing she needed was more unpleasantness. "What is it?"

Colin shook his head. "I think maybe we'd better be alone for this. I don't think you'd like this overheard."

Tessa did not care for this, fearing it would get back to Jonathan, but her curiosity was unleashed and she knew that Colin would not be deliberately melodramatic. Tessa rose and walked out of the room, leaving Colin to follow her. She did not look for an anteroom where they might speak, but led him to a far and completely unoccupied corner of the hall, near the stairs.

"I have a friend, Matthew Lincoln. I shouldn't think you'd know him," Colin began. "He's a quiet, scholarly sort of chap who doesn't go about much in the world. He's not at all the sort that dissembles."

"He sounds a paragon," Tessa said dryly, impatient for him to get on with his information.

"Point is," Colin continued, not rising to the bait, "he paid me a visit this morning and I didn't care for what he had to say, and I should think you'll care for it even less. He's a cousin to Gillane, and on his way to town from Hastings, where he has a teaching post, he stopped for the night at Gillane Castle. It's been a time since he's seen the duke and the duke filled his ear with all of his troubles.

"Just because Matt is out of town," Colin went on, "doesn't mean he's out of touch, and he knew something about what happened with Jonathan after Constance died, but the things that Gillane said to him bothered him, and knowing that you're the new Lady Hartfield and that I'm your cousin, he thought it might be best to pass it on to me."

Tessa was conscious of a sinking feeling. "I wish *you* would pass it to me," she said, chafing with suspense.

"I shall if you stop interrupting me," Colin said, sounding injured. "It's a damnable thing. Gillane told Matt that he finally dug the information out of his attorney, who had apparently refused to tell him before, that you were the one who summoned the waiter in the hall to fetch Lady Margaret the night Hartfield had that blowup with his wife at Letty's ball. He said that Jonathan knew this and deliberately set out to marry you to save himself from being convicted by the information, with your fortune being a nice little bonus for his troubles. It's bad enough that he said these things, Tess, but Matt had the distinct impression that he was being told deliberately with the intention that he should come to town and spread the tale about."

Tessa stared at him in disbelief. This was at least one problem that she had assumed was behind her and Jonathan. The duke had tried so hard to destroy Jonathan that she knew she should not be surprised at this further attempt, but she found it completely insupportable that they should be subjected to anything further from him. She did not know what effect this would have on Jonathan and their marriage, but she could not believe it would be good.

"The thing is," Colin said, breaking in to her reverie, "that even if Gillane's nastiness fell on barren ground this time, the next time it probably will not. This is too good a story and it will spread like wildfire among the gossips. Gillane will probably tell anyone who'll listen."

"No, he will not," Tessa said fiercely.

"Well, I don't see what's to be done about it," Colin said practically. "I only told you to warn you to prepare yourself for the story when it starts about. Gillane will say what he wishes and to whom, and if there is anything that can prevent him, I don't know about it."

"He must be prevented," Tessa said firmly. "I

won't have him willfully hurting my husband or me again."

"How?"

"I don't know," Tessa admitted, "but I mean to think of something."

"I wish you might, but I wouldn't wager a groat on it," Colin said gloomily. "Maybe I shouldn't have told you. You have that look you had in your eye the day you dragged me to Newgate, and I don't want you going off on any more corkbrained schemes."

"I do not consider my marraige a corkbrained scheme," Tessa said coolly, and walked past him back to the main saloon. She left shortly afterward and spent the better part of the remainder of the night deep in thought.

The following day she again awoke with hope but more of a determined nature than optimistic. Immediately after breakfast she sent a note around to her cousin and then changed and went to help her mother, as she had promised.

The morning passed more uncomfortably than she had expected, because in addition to putting up with her own impatience, there were her sister and mother to contend with, the former in a foul mood and the latter inclined to be peevish. Letitia found fault with every one of Tessa's suggestions, until Tessa, goaded, informed her that if Letitia did not wish her help Tessa would gladly relinquish any right to have a hand in the plans. It was this daunting prospect and the annoyance of her quibbling daughters that made the usually placid Lady Frances peevish. She advised Letitia, whom she correctly identified as the source of their problem, that her presence at this stage in the preparation was more of a hindrance than a help.

Letitia took great umbrage at this and declared that if she were so unappreciated she would as soon go shopping to match some ribbons for a bonnet in any case. Though it meant losing another pair of hands and a memory to sort out who must be placed next to whom at the wedding breakfast, neither Lady Frances nor Tessa minded in the least, for without friction, their task moved very quickly indeed.

"I think we are finally ahead," Lady Frances said about an hour later with a sigh of mingled relief and satisfaction. "We need only work out the last of where we wish the flowers to go, and there is no need for that until a day or two before the wedding, so I think we may safely put it off for a bit."

"Don't be too sanguine, Mamma," Tessa warned with a quizzing smile.

"If I am wrong, I know I need only put on my helpless face and call for my daughter to take pity on me," Lady Frances replied good-naturedly. The last few weeks had seen between her and Tessa the development of a closer relationship than they had yet enjoyed. With Tessa gone from the house, her virtues and talents were the more perceived for their absence, and Letitia, behaving more tiresomely than was her wont, heightened the contrast between the personalities of the two young women. Lady Frances stood and shook the creases from her dress. "I shan't keep you any longer, my love. You have been kind enough to your mamma for one day."

"If you don't mind, Mamma, I would like to stay here a bit longer," Tessa said. "I left a message for Colin to meet me here this morning as soon as he could get away, and I'd hoped he'd be here by now."

"Is something the matter, Tess?" Lady Frances asked with a small frown of concern.

"No," Tessa responded a bit too quickly. In spite of the improvement in their relationship, she was not in the habit of confiding in her mother and would have felt awkward doing so. "At least," she added for the sake of honesty, "it is nothing of any moment. Just a little problem I need Colin's help to work out."

Lady Frances' frown deepened. "You are a woman grown, Tess," she said after a few moments' hesitation, "and I would not presume to question your judgment, but I think I must say that it will not do to maintain the closeness that you once enjoyed with your cousin. There are few mates who I think truly understand it and it may well cause problems for you one day. If you are in any difficulty, your husband must be your natural choice for advice."

Tessa understood the spirit the advice was meant in and did not take it as interference. "I do understand, Mamma. You needn't worry. If anything comes between Jonathan and me it won't be Colin."

Lady Frances realized that her daughter did not mean to confide in her and allowed the matter to drop. Pleading the need to consult with her housekeeper, she left Tessa to wait for her cousin. It was another full hour before he was finally shown into the room where Tessa was waiting, trying to keep her concentration from straying from the book that was open in her lap.

"I'd hoped you'd be here sooner," she said as soon as she had greeted him.

"So did I," he concurred. "I've been in a pelter since I received your note. You made it sound as if your divorce were imminent and Hartfield should be hung by the end of the month. But I fancy you wouldn't be looking in such fine frame if either were true, so what the devil is this all about?"

She made him sit down beside her on the sofa and then outlined the plan that she had formed in the earlier hours of the morning and which she meant to be carried out as quickly as possible. It was simple enough. It required nothing more than a three-hour journey each way to Gillane Castle, with Colin to bear her company and give her the support of his presence.

"Your attic's to let," Colin said bluntly when she was done. "What the devil do you suppose you'd be able to say to Gillane to persuade him to hold his tongue? There was nothing and no one that could muzzle him before."

"He will at the very least listen to what I have to say to him," Tessa said patiently. "I think that once he hears me, he will not be anxious to spread his ruin the way that he has in the past, not when it could touch him as well."

"What is it you have to say to him?"

"I can't tell you, Colin. Please don't tease me to do so," she said regretfully, for she knew that if she did tell him all, he would much more easily trust in her success and be willing to aid her. "The principal value of what I know is that I am only one of a very few people who do know it, and I think it is a thing that the duke will not wish made public at any cost. Please trust me in this, Colin. I *could* go alone to Gillane, but I should be most uncomfortable doing so."

"I should think so!" Colin said emphatically. "Gillane's touched in his upperworks, if you ask me. *I* shouldn't care to face him alone."

"If you come with me, I won't have to," Tessa pointed out. "But don't suppose that if you refuse me, I shan't do it, for I mean to stop Gillane in any way I can, and this is the only thing I know that has the least chance of succeeding."

"I don't believe anything can succeed," Colin said, shaking his head. "I know you mean well, Tess, but this is a harebrained scheme. Wait until Hartfield returns from Cheltenham and decide with him what is best done. Gillane has no quarrel with you."

"And you do not think I should do what I can to help and protect my husband?"

"Of course you should," answered Colin, a defensive note coming into his voice. He was beginning to have a beleaguered feeling that was not unfamiliar to him when engaged in a conflict of wills with his cousin. Just so had the discussion begun when she had come to him asking him to procure the special license, and though the principal reason he had given in to her then was her pregnancy, he knew that she must have prevailed in any case. Her will was the stronger, and when she *would* have her way, she generally did. "But you must do so sensibly and not go dashing off on mad schemes that will as like as not make matters worse rather than better."

"If Jonathan and I have to go through any more scandal over his first marriage, I don't believe things would have the least chance of being worse," she insisted. "I could not bear it, Colin, and nor do I think my marriage could. I would prefer it if Jonathan never even knew of this new threat to his . . . to our happiness."

He saw that she meant this and would truly carry out her plan even if he refused to aid her. This, he thought, would be worse than abetting her, for he did have doubt of the duke's sanity, at least as far as Hartfield was concerned. "Very well," he said, capitulating. "If you'd rather have me than Hartfield in this, then we'll do the thing. We'll have to go in your carriage, though. I've only brought my curricle up with me from Boxwood."

"I'll send a message to have my traveling chaise prepared at once," she said. "It will be much more comfortable for the journey than my town carriage."

"It can't be today, I have things to take care of this afternoon. We'll have to . . ." He broke off as Letitia came into the room.

Letitia gave one and then the other a speaking glance. "Planning your elopement?" she asked archly. "It seems to me that if you'd wanted Colin you might have had him at any time without causing such a sensation with Hartfield first."

"Go away, Letty," Tessa said, annoyed. "I haven't time for your nonsense now."

"Obviously. You have assignations to plan and to keep. Does Hartfield know what you are about, or have I walked in on a guilty secret?" she asked with a knowing smile. "I shan't keep you. I only wanted the copy of *La Belle Assemblée* that I left in here this morning." She walked past them to a nearby table and found what she wished. She started to leave the room but turned and added, "Frankly, Tess, I can't say that I blame you for having changed your mind about Jonathan. I think he is an abominable man. But if you *do* mean to do anything outrageous like elope with a clergyman who also happens to be your first cousin, it had better not be until after my wedding. I won't have you casting me in the shade again."

This last was said with heavy warning, and Tessa sighed with impatience. "You know perfectly well that Colin and I are not planning a secret rendezvous. It is a private matter that has nothing to do with you and won't interfere with your precious wedding in any way. Does that satisfy you?"

"If it's true," Letitia said musingly. "I wonder, though, why you thought enough to tell me this—you aren't usually so careful of my feelings or opinion. I think it is to keep me from investigating further. It is something indiscreet in some way and you would as lief I didn't know of it."

"Quite right," Tessa concurred, unperturbed by what Letitia had thought was a great point scored over her sister. "And I will thank you to leave us and forget whatever you may have heard, or I may *just* elope to spite your wedding."

Letitia gave Tessa a brief sardonic smile in answer. "I have it on good authority that husbands take a very dim view of secret rendezvous with exceptionally handsome young men when related to their wives. I can't think Jonathan will like this at all if he hears of it." This was a clear threat, and on its final note she turned again and left the room.

"Vixen!" Colin said with feeling. "Well, that tears it. We shall have to give up the scheme now."

"Why?"

"We couldn't bring the thing off now that that minx has wind of it. She'll tell Hartfield for certain."

"Let her," Tessa said recklessly. "It'll be an accomplished thing by the time that Jonathan returns from Cheltenham, for I don't expect him until the evening at the latest. You know what men are at prizefights, and there are few who feel up to an early start. He may possibly be gone another day in any case. I own I wish we might start at once, and do the thing today, but if we start early tomorrow, we will be back well before dinner."

"He still won't like it when she tells him," Colin persisted, "even if you succeed, which I take leave to doubt. Likely as not he'll blame me for not stopping you," he added gloomily, "as if I could! I'll wager you don't get around him the way you do me."

"That is why I am married to him and not you," Tessa said tartly, and then, because she did not wish to offend him and cause him to change his mind, added, "He will as likely be grateful to you for standing my protector. I do thank you, Colin; it would be so much more difficult without you. Do you think you could be ready by nine tomorrow morning?"

Colin sighed and supposed he could, and the last of the details for the travel were arranged between them.

Tessa called for Colin on the next morning at a few minutes before nine, to receive the vexing information that he was already gone out to attend to unexpected work. Tessa at first expected that this was a ploy to force her to change her hands, but the servant who gave her this information assured her that Mr. McAffe expected to be only a little delayed and would soon be home.

Tessa was not particularly put out by this, for she had deliberately set so early a time for a journey that covered little more than three hours to allow for delays and setbacks. The only thing in this that signified to her in their traveling plans was that she return to town before Jonathan, and she was not yet concerned for this in any way.

Unhappily, she had not thought to provide herself with a book or newspaper to ease her wait, and after the first quarter-hour or so of waiting, the time became rather heavy. As it continued to pass and nearly an hour had gone by without a sight of or word from Colin, she began once again to suspect him of subterfuge. She was of a mind to give up her wait and go on without him when she finally saw McAffe coming down the street at a brisk walk. Tessa had elected to wait within the carriage, and he came directly to it and got in.

"I'm sorry, Tess," he apologized at once. "This really couldn't be helped."

"It doesn't signify," she said untruthfully, and told the coachman to go on. The comfortable edge she had given them to obtain an interview with Gillane and be back before dinner had nearly evaporated, but displaying her irritation to Colin would be to no good purpose.

Their journey was uneventful and they made good time, but to Tessa, who was at one and the same time anxious to have it over with and dreading what she must face at the end of it, it seemed in some ways too long and in others too short. Both Colin and Tessa being preoccupied with their thoughts on the immediate future, the conversation between them was desultory.

Because of the delay, Tessa had instructed the coachman to put the horses along at a good pace, deciding that even a stop for a change would be better to save time than a more leisurely pace to save the horses for the whole journey. They were less than a half-hour away from Gillane Castle when that stop became necessary.

The carriage came to a rattling halt on the cobblestones of the Stag and Rabbit, a coaching inn a few miles short of the turnoff to the lesser road that would eventually take them to Gillane Bower and the castle.

Colin suggested that they get down for a minute to stretch their legs and perhaps have a bit of refreshment to ease the dryness of travel, but Tessa vetoed this.

Taking his courage in both hands, Colin sighed and said abruptly, "I can't let you do this thing, Tess."

"What?"

"I said, I can't let you do this."

"I know what you said," Tessa said in a voice that was both astonished and caustic. "I could not believe that I heard you say it. Do you realize that we are nearly there?"

"Yes, and that's why I am bringing this to a halt now. My mind is made up to this, Tess. It won't do you the least good to try to bully me out of it. We are going to turn around and go home."

"I haven't come this far to turn tail now!"

"It isn't that, it's just good sense." His tone was calm and firm. "To aid and abet you in a thing that I believe to be wrong and may well be harmful to you and even to your husband and marriage would be dishonorable in any gentleman; to one of my profession it must be unconscionable."

"Oh, very pretty," Tessa said bitterly. "You choose now to be overcome with an excess of piety. This could be the saving of my marriage, not the ruining of it, and I must be the best judge of what is necessary. You needn't fear that you will have to take any part in it; you can even stay in the carriage if you like."

"I'm not going to Gillane and neither are you," he said in a hard voice. He pushed down the window and called to the ostlers who were backing the new team into the shafts. He informed them that they were stopping after all and would not need the team for a bit. One of the men came over at once and let down the steps for them.

"We are not stopping, Colin," Tessa said dangerously.

"We are."

"Perhaps you are. I am going on."

"You are getting out of this carriage with me, Tess. I'm dashed if I care what manner of fuss it makes if I have to force you."

Colin could not know of Jonathan's suspicions, but he said the one thing that gave her pause. She was familiar with this inn and knew that it catered almost exclusively to the quality and was well-patronized. They might not be recognized in the common way, but if there were a scene made in such a well-known place, the story would undoubtedly pass among the members of the ton and ultimately reach Jonathan.

It was one thing to tell him that she had had Colin's help if the mission was successful, but it would be quite another should he discover what she had done and she have nothing to show for it.

Colin saw by her expression that his point had gone home. "Come, now, Tess," he said, prepared to be handsome now that he had won his point. "You're the most sensible female I know. You'll see once you've discussed this thing with Hartfield that I was in the right of it. We'll have a bit of lemonade and biscuits before we go on, shall we?"

Tessa had lost this round, but she by no means considered the battle at an end, and conceded no victory. "You might at least have told me that you would not help while we were still in town, and saved us this useless journey," she said angrily.

"Now, I couldn't, could I?" he replied reasonably. "I know you, Tess. You would have just gone off without me, leaving me blithering on the pavement."

Tessa gave him a long look. "I would like to leave you blithering in the courtyard right now."

But Colin knew she was just venting her anger and frustration, and with a small indulgent smile that Tessa found utterly infuriating, he got out of the carriage and turned to help her down. She accepted this courtesy meekly enough and followed him across the courtyard and into the inn without so much as a glare to show her displeasure. Colin congratulated himself on the firm position he had taken, and his courage in facing down his strong-willed cousin.

Tessa stood quietly beside him while he procured for them a small parlor, then entered it and sat down without any demure. She watched expressionlessly while Colin pulled out a chair from the table and sat down, stretching his long legs.

"I'm glad you're being sensible," he said. "You'll see I'm right, too, when you think on this for a bit."

Tessa gave a deep and resigned sigh. "I suppose," she admitted reluctantly, "but I did so wish that I might have taken care of this matter without Jonathan even knowing of it. I suppose that . . ." She broke off, appearing to look about her for something. "I must have left my reticule in the carriage," she said after a few moments.

Colin straightened. "I'll get it."

"No, I placed it under the seat in a special way as a precaution against highwaymen," she said. "I know it is silly, but I always do it. I'll find it myself."

"Ho!" said Colin with a snort. "I'm awake on that suit, my girl. You'll wait here and I'll go to the carriage."

"Don't be foolish, Colin," Tessa said, exasperated. "If I was going to go on to Gillane, I would never have left the carriage in the first place. I never really meant to go to him alone anyway; I just said that to make you wish to come with me." She had risen and walked to the door as she spoke. She put her hand on the door and turned to him. "When the waiter comes back, would you see if they have sugar cakes? I would particularly like that."

Though Colin did not completely trust her, he supposed it was safe enough, for the horses had been removed from the shafts and if she was gone for more than a few minutes, he could easily run out to see what she was about. In any case, he was used to taking the path of least resistance with Tessa.

He got up slowly and went over to the window which overlooked the courtyard. He could just see the corner of her chaise where it had been led to one side to await their need for it again. He could not, from where he stood, see her enter the carriage, but he saw it move slightly and supposed it was her.

Two vehicles, each approaching from a different direction, came into the courtyard at that moment, and at once, all before Colin was a beehive of activity. Ostlers appeared from every corner of the courtyard as if by magic and horses were brought out from the stables at a trot. It was always a fascinating sight to see well-trained ostlers effect a quick change of teams; they did so with an ease and rapidity that was enviable.

The dust had barely settled about the wheels of the carriages before first one was off and then the other. Colin smiled to himself, abstractly pleased with the efficiency of the place. He casually glanced again in the direction of their own carriage, and saw to his horror, dismay, and utter astonishment that it was no longer where he had last seen it.

With a sharp intake of breath, he whirled away from the window and across the parlour. He was out of the inn and standing in the courtyard in the space of a moment, but there was no sign at all of Tessa or the traveling chaise.

Colin could scarcely credit the evidence of his eyes, or rather, he did not wish to believe he had been so duped.

But whether he believed it or not was clearly

immaterial. Tessa was gone and there was nothing at all left for him to do but return to the parlour to partake of the lemonade and cakes while he profitlessly berated himself for his gullibility and wondered yet again how it was that his cousin had managed to have her way when he had been so determined that she should not.

Chapter Ten

Letitia did not give a great deal of thought to the conversation she had overheard between Colin and Tessa until she recalled later that evening that her brother-in-law was away from town. Though it was a while since she had been actively angry with either Tessa or Jonathan, she had far from forgotten her grievances with both. The lionization of Jonathan after his acquittal and triumphant return to the bosom of society had tapered off, and so had the excessive (in her opinion) attention that both had received.

Though her sister's dashing new style had won for her many admirers and copiers, Letitia was once again fussed over and admired enough for her not to begrudge Tessa her own court. There was no reason now to suppose that her wedding would not be the big social occasion that Letitia wished it to be, and if she would not after all take precedence over her sister, it was hardly a thing to hold a grudge for.

Her current feelings for Jonathan were quite a different matter. She felt he had deliberately tried to make her look the fool, and this she did not easily forgive. Though it was not her way to brood on a means of revenge, Letitia could be quite nasty when she chose, and she was not likely to pass up an opportunity when one was presented to her.

Letitia knew, of course, that there was no question at all of there being any truth to her nonsensical suggestion that Colin and Tessa might elope, but she had more than once observed a look she imagined was disapproving in her brother-in-law's eyes when they were upon Tessa and Colin in conversation. Her vanities did not impair her perception where other people were concerned, and she fancied that Jonathan might without much difficulty be brought to jealousy.

She had no notion of making any true trouble between the couple; she did not suppose for a moment that whatever the plans of Colin and Tessa were, they would not be perfectly innocent, and in fact her scheme was to make Jonathan look the fool.

If her plan was truly a success, he would go after them, and when he found them together in whatever blameless thing they were engaged in, he would make complete cake of himself over the matter. She felt the delicious anticipation of vengeance achieved when she wondered how long it would take his quick mind to realize that he had been deliberately set up by the sister-in-law he had treated so poorly.

Letitia did not know what time Jonathan would be returning, nor did she know when Tessa and Colin meant to be away, and she could only hope that it would not be until Jonathan had returned. At just about the time that Colin was entering the carriage before they set out, Letitia set out for Upper Mount Street, intending to see if a little subtle prying could coax from her sister a bit more of her plans.

It therefore vexed her very much to be told at the door that Lady Hartfield was from home, but the information that his lordship had just this moment returned from Cheltenham was most welcome, and Letitia knew instinctively that she had been led here at this time by a sort of natural timing. She felt a tiny thrill of joy that Jonathan's comeuppance might actually be at hand.

It was on the tip of Jonathan's tongue to deny himself to his sister-in-law. He had not dipped as deeply the night before as his wife had supposed he would, and, anxious to get an early start, he had started back to town at nearly dawn. He had not slept well, for all his abstinence, and this and the long, early drive had left him abnormally weary.

But his impulsive behavior with Letitia had already caused more than enough trouble in his life, and he saw no point in giving additional offense to his sister-in-law—whom he had already guessed suspected his motives and behavior of that day—when the cost to him was not more than a few minutes of his time. Whatever Letitia wished to see him about, he could deal with it summarily if tactfully.

"I didn't suppose you would be home so early this day," Letitia said as she came into the saloon where he had elected to meet her. "Tess told me that you'd gone to that stupid, vulgar prizefight that has made the company so thin of gentlemen for the last few days."

"It took place yesterday," he said, and without further explanation added, "And now I am home. I am sorry that Tessa is not here for you. You would not have an idea where she may be, would you? I was told by the servants that she left about an hour or so ago in the traveling chaise but without informing anyone of her destination. Is there a connexion of yours not far from town that she might be visiting?"

Jonathan's innocent question played exactly into Letitia's hands. It was obvious that Tess had already left on her errand with Colin, and that if she chose her words carefully, she might indeed be able to cause Jonathan to react as she would wish.

"Oh, dear!" she cried in dramatic accents, artfully allowing her reticule to slip through her slender fingers. "I had hoped to be in time to prevent this. I came to try to talk poor Tess to sense, but I see that I am too late."

Jonathan regarded his sister-in-law balefully, in no humor for Letitia's playacting. "I consider sense one of Tessa's principal assets," he said dampeningly. "I think you have no need for concern on that head." He bent and picked up her fallen purse and handed it to her.

Letitia regarded him with her exquisite blue eyes filled with loving pity. "You have no notion of it, do you?" she asked with gentle sadness.

"Apparently not," he said briskly, stifling an impatient sigh. "What are you speaking of?"

Letitia turned her face from him as if she could not bear to look at him as she spoke. "I feared how it would be. I have always known that you and Tessa . . . It must be discomfiting for me to mention it, but I have always known that your marriage was one of convenience. I am so blessed in Walter that I had hoped that you and she—"

"I will thank you not to presume a knowledge of my marriage that you do not possess," he said coldly. He had no intention of discussing Tessa with her, and if the only way he could prevent it was bluntness, then so it would be.

"I know where she is now, and that is no presumption," Letitia said waspishly, stung by his tone. "Where?"

"With Colin." She saw from beneath her lashes that he had visibly tensed. "It is not certain, but it is possible that they have eloped."

He actually and infuriatingly smiled. "Nonsense."

"If only it were!" she said mournfully. "I overheard them planning. Tessa agreed to call for him in the carriage and Colin actually said that he was only doing this because she clearly preferred him to you. They have always been so close; given your loveless marriage, this was inevitable. It is such a great pity for you to be cast once again into a scandal broth,

and a pity Tessa could not know her own mind
before that became necessary."

"I don't know what this absurdity is, Letty," he
said with steel in his voice, "but I don't think even
you really believe that Tess has eloped. Perhaps
Tessa has not confided in you—I know she does not
wish it generally known yet—but she is breeding. I
think the most erstwhile lover would find an increasing mistress more a hindrance than a pleasure on an
illicit flight."

"Even if it is his child?" Letitia said spitefully,
furious that her scheme might fail. The color drained
from his face and his eyes nearly blazed with a
sudden rage that made Letitia suddenly desirous of
qualifying her remark. "I don't know such a thing,
of course, but I don't know what else to think, for I
did hear them planning to go off somewhere together,
and it was to be surreptitious, because when I asked
Tess about it in all innocence, she told me that the
matter was private and I was to forget that I had
ever heard it mentioned."

"And from there you let your imagination have
rein," he said with biting contempt. "I neither know
nor care what you think you have overheard, but I
know my wife is not eloping with McAffe or anyone.
If there is to be any degree of harmony in this
family, I trust you will not again repeat what you
have just said to me. I, in my turn, will refrain from
informing Torrance of your behavior in your father's
bookroom. Yours is something more than a match of
convenience, and I don't doubt he has witnessed
just that degree of flirtation between us to give it
credence."

"You would not do a thing so dishonorable," Letitia gasped.

"What you are doing is honorable?" he said with
an unmistakable sneer.

Letitia could scarcely believe that her scheme had
failed so signally. "You are making a mistake,

Hartfield," she told him, nearly stamping her foot with frustration. "Even if they are not eloping, they have gone off on a secret assignation, and if you don't believe me, why don't you see if you can find Colin now? I'd wager half my dowry that you could not."

"Very likely," he replied with a maddening want of concern. "They probably have gone off together on the accomplishment of some errand. Cut line, Letty. Do you suppose I don't know why you are doing this?"

Letitia's full, dewy lips trembled with anger and the fear that she had once again made a cake of herself. "I think you are the most despicable of creatures," she said on a sob. "I only wish to help—"

"You only wish to pay me back," he said baldly. "You have realized by now that I had no intention of ravishing you that afternoon and only wished to frighten you out of attempting to set me up as one of your flirts. Perhaps the thing was ill-done of me," he conceded, "and for that I beg your pardon, but don't think to bamboozle me with feminine wiles or graces. Playacting is wasted on me."

"All feeling is wasted on your sort," she said nastily. She drew on her gloves so forcefully that she made a tear in the thumb. "I don't blame Tess for playing you false. I wish I had never tried to warn you." She gave him a long fulminating look and then left the room on a flounce which entirely destroyed the effect of injured dignity for which she was trying.

Jonathan crossed the room to a chair near the windows, and if Letitia could have seen his face at that moment, her chagrin would have changed to gloating triumph. He had hidden his true feelings from her, and at no little cost to himself.

He did not believe that Tessa was eloping with Colin, but he knew well that assignations made away from the prying eyes of the ton were not uncommon happenings.

He had nearly convinced himself in the quiet moments of the time he had been away that his fears of reliving his first marriage again were only helping to make just that come to pass. Whenever they talked more than commonplaces, they were at odds, and misunderstandings were far too frequent. The position he took at these times helped nothing, and in fact he now feared that they might actually have driven her to McAffe's arms. If the notion that she might be in her cousin's arms at all was difficult to endure, the notion that his own defensive and jealous behavior might have helped to bring it about was unbearable.

His mistake, he thought, lay in his own cravenness. Though few had credited it, his first marriage had been a love match, at least on his side, and it was his fear of pain that made him wish to settle for friendship in his new marriage with Tessa, when he knew in his heart that he wished it to be far more. The truth he had been denying was at last in front of him and would not be ignored. Tessa meant everything to him and he could not lose her as he had Constance when the hurt she had brought him had finally turned his love to indifference. He did not know if he could have changed that, but he did know that he never really tried to do so. This time he had to try, or there would be no more future for him than if he had faced the hangman's rope.

Jonathan had no idea where his wife might be, and the logical thing would be to await her return. But he could not. He convinced himself that perhaps her *affaire* with Colin was yet unconsummated; he needed to do so for his peace, and he also allowed himself to believe that he could prevent it. He went to the mews himself to have his phaeton and four made ready, and had the good luck of learning from one of the grooms, who had overheard a conversation between the coachman and the guard, at least the direction they had planned to take from the city.

It was a route that was most familiar to him and he knew that he might ask at several places along the way for them.

A quarter-hour later he was once again on the road, this time with nothing more than his own determination to keep him company.

As her chaise came to a halt in front of the magnificent facade of Gillane Castle, Tessa knew a moment of trepidation and doubt. She was as determined as ever on her course, and equally confident of its outcome, but memories of the duke, though she knew him only slightly, made her leary of the confrontation. At his best she knew his mien could be forbidding, and it was certainly a forlorn hope that she would find him at his best in this situation.

Whatever his feelings might be on beholding her, they would doubtless deteriorate even further when he discovered the purpose of her visit. But it was too late for doubts, and she was determined to do what must be done. She gathered up her skirts and allowed the guard who had put down the steps to hand her from the carriage.

There was still the possibility that the duke would simply refuse to see her, and for a moment she nearly decided to give her maiden name, but then she realized it would be pointless. He would be certain to know that she was now the new Lady Hartfield.

The impassive majordomo who had opened the door at the sounds of her arrival flicked his heavily hooded eyes when she boldly handed him her visiting card and announced her title. He glanced beyond her to the carriage for the crest which was certainly well known to him. Tessa fancied he gave her a measuring look, but could not be certain. The overt thing he did was to escort her into a small saloon to await the decision of his master to see or not see her.

Tessa removed her gloves and bonnet and settled

into a comfortable chair, expecting a considerable wait, but the butler did not tarry and was soon with her again. As unreadable as before, he requested her to follow him to the duke. Tessa was all the more surprised that the duke's decision to see her had been brought to her so quickly, as they traversed what seemed to her to be miles of corridor. She suspected that the man's own curiosity had made him quick and the number of servants whom they happened to pass as they made their progress also made her think that he had spread the word among his cohorts that the new Lady Hartfield had come to Gillane.

Tessa was only too aware that she could not match her predecessor in beauty, but she could carry herself with the dignity of any duke's daughter, and affecting regal indifference, she kept her chin high to give them all the best look they could manage.

At last they reached the room where the duke was to be found, and the butler, bowing in a manner to befit a ducal retainer, announced her and left, shutting the door behind Tessa and leaving her face to face with the man she regarded as her greatest enemy.

The room was not large, and looked to have once been a sitting room, but now it was outfitted with a large leather-topped desk that was littered with the same thing that covered nearly every bit of available wall space: maps of every shape, size, and color, some commonplace and others fantastical. In spite of the seriousness of her mission, or perhaps because of it, Tessa was drawn away from her purpose for a moment. She walked over to the wall to her left and looked closely at a map that was placed at her eye level. It was obviously quite ancient, and purported to be, from what she could make out of the Latin lettering, a view of the entire world. It was quite wrong, of course, but was so beautifully executed with two-headed monsters rising out of the seas and odd masses of uncharted lands that it was instantly arresting.

She was not aware that she was staring at it with such concentration until the duke spoke at her elbow and made her jump. She turned to see that the tall gray-haired man had entered the room and seated himself at the desk. "It is a beautiful thing, is it not?" he said in a voice that surprised Tessa with its gentleness.

"Y-yes, it is."

"It doesn't matter that it shows only a few crescent-shaped islands where the Americas should be or that India is not more that a long sail in a straight line from here; a thing so beautifully made deserves to exist despite its faults."

His dark, intently blue eyes seemed to bore into her as he spoke, and Tessa realized he was not really speaking of the map at all. She had the sudden chilling sensation that he could see into her mind and discern her purpose, but knew that it was his own fanaticism about his daughter that made him so easily able to read her. She felt more chilled than if he had been able to see into her mind. For the first time since she had left Colin behind at the Stag and Rabbit, she wished that she had taken the time to persuade Colin to accompany her instead of going off on her own on impulse.

"Please sit down, Lady Hartfield," he invited her. "I won't ask if you would like refreshment for I am certain this is not a social call. In case we should not be so amiable by the end of our interview, I'll tell you now that I think you are a woman of spirit. You not only marry that worthless moneygrubber with the sad example of my daughter before you, you come here to me, which I think in some ways was the braver of the two acts. Why are you here?"

That was plain speaking, yet Tessa realized she too preferred that there be no amenities. "I have come to do what I can to prevent you from spread-

ing any more of your complaints against my husband.
I think that he—and I, too—have suffered quite
enough in this matter. Whatever your feelings for
Jonathan, he has been exonerated of all guilt in the
death of your daughter, and it is not right that you
should continue to abuse him in such a way."

The duke did not pretend to misunderstand her.
"What is not right," he said with a hardness coming
into his voice, "is that my beautiful girl lies in her
grave while he is allowed the freedom to marry yet
another heiress and continue his infamy. You, Lady
Hartfield, are just his next victim. You should be
coming to me as a friend, not a critic."

"I might if I believed that Jonathan had anything
to do with your daughter's death," she said without
hesitation, "but if I believed that, I would not have
married him at all. I have been told that you have
discovered I was the woman who sent the waiter to
fetch Lady Margaret to Constance. That is quite true.
But Jonathan neither seduced me nor forced me into
marriage with him. It was, in fact, I who wished to
marry him and he who did so with reservation. He
felt that the world would feel as you do, that he is a
fortune hunter. You are mistaken."

"My Connie thought that at first," he said mean-
ingfully.

"I do not know all the details of my husband's
marriage to your daughter," Tessa said, braving the
lion, "but I was reasonably well-acquainted with your
daughter, and though I know it will give you great
offense, I am compelled to tell you that I do not
believe the failure of it lay with Jonathan. Constance
was lovely but spoiled, charming but selfish."

All of the duke's remaining amiability evaporated
at these words, and this was clear from his expression.
"If you have come to criticize my daughter in defense of your husband, and supposed that by this I
would be persuaded not to let the world know what
manner of man Jonathan Hartfield is, I fear you have

come on a fool's errand and can only wonder at your lack of sense."

There was a definite hint of menace in his tone, and Colin's strictures that her bluntness might make the duke even more determined to ruin Jonathan haunted her, but it was impossible to turn back now. "What brought me here," she said with a coolness that she was far from feeling, "was the need to inform you that slander can be a game for two players." She saw the duke stiffen, but went on, "I know why Constance was so distraught those last days of her life and what it was between them that made her and Jonathan argue so. I did overhear their conversation the night of my sister's ball and I know that he meant to divorce her and that there was nothing that was going to dissuade him from this. He didn't give a tinker's damn any longer for her fortune, her beauty, or even what a divorce would do to his name that his wife's behavior had not already done. She was breeding, your grace, and the child was not his; he would not acknowledge it or give it his name."

Her words might not have been spoken, for all the visible effect they had on the duke, and for a moment she feared that he had known the truth and that her information was valueless. His eyes were still rock hard, his features had not moved a hairbreadth. But all at once there was a perceptible sag in the whole of his person that made him a suddenly less menacing person. Gillane, though, was no man to be counted down for a single blow.

"You damned lying bitch," he thundered, standing suddenly in a startling way. "You *dare* to come here to me and say these things of my girl. Jealous strumpet! You were his doxy, weren't you, before he ever came to town that night? You planned it between you, knowing you could use your father to get him off should anything go wrong." He seemed to tower above her, but Tessa had herself in command and did not flinch, though his voice was a roar in her ears. "I should have had the dogs set on your carriage the moment I heard who it was. I won't slander you, madam, I shall destroy you and that thieving, murdering husband of yours. You may depend upon it."

Colin's pessimistic prediction that she would only make matters worse seemed to have borne fruit, but Tessa was not yet ready to give up. "You are speaking nonsense and you know it," she said firmly and without a trace of tremor, though inside she was far from calm.

The duke's complexion was becoming alarmingly florid and his breathing was rapid and very audible. Even as she met his eyes unquakingly, his color suddenly faded to the opposite extreme and he swayed slightly.

"My lord duke!" she cried in alarm, and rose quickly to help him into his chair. "Are you well? Should I call for one of your servants?"

He pushed her roughly aside and sat down as if his legs had given up his support. A sudden feeling of overwhelming pity came over Tessa as she saw the duke, not as a formidable enemy, but as an old and rather sad man. She knew she had nothing to fear from him, at least physically, and without hesitation resumed her seat.

"If I call for one of my men, it will be to have you whipped from the house," he said viciously. "Your sex will no longer protect you here. You know, don't you, that you have given me the proof I need that Hartfield did kill my girl? He did not want the disgrace of that divorce, he killed her as the easiest way out of his dilemma."

"If anything, it proves Constance's motive for taking the laudanum herself," Tessa said in answer. "It doesn't matter what you think, for there is nothing you could do now except to spread your verbal poison, and if you do, I promise you this: I shall personally see to it that its virulence rounds upon you and does you in as well. I shall tell anyone and everyone who will listen just what manner of slut your daughter was and the disgrace she had finally brought herself to."

"If this is true," the duke said suddenly in a controlled voice, "why didn't Hartfield himself publish the thing? He did not dare, for he knew it would convict him."

"He would not have it convict Constance," Tessa said quietly. "In spite of all she had done to him, he could not bring himself, even when she was not alive to feel her disgrace, to destroy what little reputation she had remaining to her. But Constance is nothing to me. I don't give a damn for her name or your feelings. Jonathan will not like it, but I would rather face his anger than see him ruined. You won't stop me and you shan't be able to fight my innuendos any more than Jonathan could battle successfully against yours."

The duke's expression was so furious that Tessa feared he would fall into an apoplexy. But once again his high color receded, and a slow smile spread across his lined features. "I begin to see why Hartfield was attracted to you. You are very like her in some ways. You won't escape any more than she did. He drove her to it and he'll do the same to you."

"Do you mean he drove her to kill herself?" Tessa asked, startled by his words.

The duke nodded and at last removed his fierce gaze from her. "He didn't love her; my girl needed love. That's why she went after other men, and it is as much his fault that she died as if he'd given her that dose with his hands."

"Then you know he did not do so?" Tessa asked carefully.

But the duke only harkened to thoughts of his own. "My sweet girl cried. Night after night she cried. I would stand in the hall and listen to her. I tried to give her comfort, but this time she would not even talk to me. I see now why she couldn't; she wouldn't have wanted me to know this." He looked up at Tessa and she saw his eyes were bright with unshed tears. "May God forgive you for telling me," he added in a fierce whisper.

"May He forgive us both for making it necessary," Tessa responded quietly.

Gillane went on as if she hadn't spoken, and was in fact speaking to himself, having nearly forgotten her presence. "I saw what she was about and I never made a push to stop her." He broke down completely then, burying his face in his hands and making a low keening noise that chilled Tessa to the bone.

Tessa, with one of her instinctive insights, knew that the duke would never again be a bother to her or Jonathan. He would not speak of Jonathan's culpability again, not just for fear of her own threat, but because he understood the truth at last.

Tessa left him without speaking again, and returned unescorted through the twisting corridors, hoping she would not lose her way. She only wished to be free of this unhappy house with as little delay as possible.

Jonathan did not mean to stop at the Stag and Rabbit. Because of its popularity and nearness to Gillane, he was well-known there and there was another place a bit farther along the road where he might ask after the travelers and be less conspicuous. But he had held his team to a clipping pace and they were beginning to flag. He knew that the job horses to be had at the Stag and Rabbit were superior to the usual sort found on the road.

He drove into the courtyard and remained in the carriage while his team was removed from the traces and another put in their place. The head ostler came over to him at a signal, touching his forelock in recognition. On impulse, Jonathan asked after Tessa's carriage, supposing that she too might have chosen here to make a change.

The ostler, whose observant powers had from time to time supplemented his income on this busy post road, prided himself on his powers of recollection. But this time he had no need to tax his memory; the odd circumstances of the carriage arriving and being pulled aside and then going off again with just the lady, and the sight of the crest with which he was most familiar, recalled it to him at once.

"Aye, m'lord," he said. "Came in not more than half-hour ago. Changed the team and was gone again after a bit. But if you are looking to find where it has gone, maybe that gentleman her ladyship let off here could tell you that. Far as I know, he ain't gone off again."

Jonathan was so startled by this information that he nearly betrayed himself by asking the ostler whom he was speaking of, but collecting himself, he thanked the man, gave into his hands a generous number of coins and the reins of his team. Perhaps the man had mistaken the crest, but he decided to see "the gentleman" for himself anyway. Just to see what if anything it would produce, he gave the landlord Colin's name and, to his surprise, was shown at once into the parlour where Colin had been cooling his heels since Tessa had abandoned him at the inn.

Colin's back was to the door, but when he heard Jonathan enter the room he wheeled about half-expecting it to be Tessa come to her senses and come to fetch him back to London. The peal he meant to ring over her was well-rehearsed by now, and an angry frown marred his handsome features, but this changed rather quickly to a wide-eyed stare as he stood astonished at the sight of Jonathan. "Hartfield!"

he exclaimed as if observing a shade instead of a man. "How the devil do you—?"

"Come to be here?" Jonathan interjected silkily. "I do not think that is nearly as germane as how it is that you are here. Where is Tess?"

"You look as if your next question will be to ask me to name my friends," Colin said unhappily, "and I'll tell you now, I won't do it. That wife of yours is as headstrong as her sister and meant to have her way in this whatever I would say, so if you don't like the thing, don't look to me for the blame."

"I should not think of calling you to account," Jonathan said with a contemptuous curl of his lips. "One may only do so honorably with another gentleman. My regret is that I did not think to bring my horsewhip inside with me."

Colin caught his breath. "Damn you, Hartfield!" he said, goaded into the obscenity. "You may not like what I've done, but you've no right to speak to me in such a way, and I damn well won't have it."

"Ah, you've rediscovered your manhood," Jonathan said with mock approval. "I began to think that my wife had been deceived by a man-milliner."

Colin actually gasped at this, but as he surveyed the furious visage of the man who stood across from him in a stance that could only be called challenging, his excellent mind began to put his words and manner together and began to suspect the truth. "Good Lord, Hartfield," he said, astonished. "You don't think . . . Yes, I can see that you do. Damn it, man, don't be absurd. Tessa is like one of my sisters, only the truth is, I like her better. The only designs I have on the person of your lovely wife is that I should like to wring her neck. She dragged me out here against my will and abandoned me when she couldn't persuade me to go along with her harebrained scheme." Seeing the hesitation come into Jonathan's expression, he added. "You may not care for this story when I tell it to you, but you'll mind it a deal less than the one you are imagining now."

Jonathan was not prepared to give his rival any quarter, but if nothing else, it *was* obvious that Tessa had left him here and gone on somewhere without him, which was hardly loverlike behavior. He relaxed his threatening posture and came farther into the room. "Very well, McAffe; I'll listen."

Colin let loose an audible sigh of relief. "If you hadn't had my skin, the archbishop would have. Rather frowns on having his secretaries caught up in compromising situations with the wives of men inclined to be hot off the pistol. Not," he added hastily, "that either Tess or I am compromised in any way, but if you took your pound of flesh, well, how would it look? Please sit down, Hartfield."

Jonathan did so, and Colin followed suite, continuing, "I am not a coward, whatever you may think, but I am by nature and profession a man of peace, and frankly it makes me nervous to have you come rampaging in here like a dashed Visigoth ready to take up your battleax." A reluctant hint of a smile touched Jonathan's lips, and Colin was a bit heartened. "I know that you will think me a fool for letting her push me into this mess, but say what you will, Tessa has always been able to talk me around to her way of thinking since we were in the cradle together. I don't know why I thought I could prevail if I stood firm, for you see what it has gotten me." He then went on to tell Jonathan everything that had occurred since his conversation with Tessa at the party the night before had sparked in her the idea of coming to Gillane.

Jonathan heard him out, and at the end of it, over a shared glass or two of wine, the men came to a better understanding. Each found himself more pleased with the other than he had ever been before. "I'd best go after her," Jonathan said presently.

"Gillane won't do her a physical injury, but an interview with him can have its own pains."

The distance to Gillane was not far and was easily covered by the four horses pulling the light phaeton. As he pulled between the gates, offering a quick salute to an astounded gatekeeper, he was assailed by more feeling than he would have supposed he would have for the place. Gillane Castle had been his home and refuge, a substitute for his own lost estate. Later, it had been the place where he had come to escape all the things in his marriage which had given him pain. If he felt some anger as he sped along the straight drive, he felt mostly regret and the hope that this was at least one lesson which he had well-learned.

It had been some time since more than one carriage in the space of a morning had come up the sweep in front of the great manse, and once again it was the butler himself who made the push to greet the new arrival, but when he saw who it was, he looked completely thunderstruck. "M-my lord," he gasped, and wondered at the events that were unfolding on this day.

"Good afternoon, Kerwick," Jonathan said, unperturbed. "I understand my wife is here; if she is with the duke, I wish you to take me to them at once."

"I . . . I can't, my lord," the majordomo stammered. "That is, it would be as much as my job was worth if I did." He was uncomfortable and studiously avoided Jonathan's eyes. It went against his grain to say these things to the man he had nearly regarded in the light of master of the castle, since the duke had lived so much in town. "You must know what his grace's feelings are toward you," he added unhappily.

"Only too well," Jonathan said grimly. "And that is why I do not wish my wife to be in his exclusive company. She came here on the mistaken assumption that Gillane is a man who can be dealt with in a reasonable manner. She is not so much foolish as innocent, and I won't allow her to be subjected to the abuse which he has called down upon me."

Kerwick understood what Lord Hartfield was saying to him and agreed completely. He wrestled with his own best interests and his sympathy for a man who he, too, believed had suffered quite enough. Without speaking a word, he moved a step aside, but Jonathan too understood and quickly entered the vaulted entrance hall. "The map room, my lord," Kerwick said barely above a whisper as he passed him.

Jonathan ascended the wide marble stairs as quickly as he could without running, and had only reached the top when he saw his wife coming toward him from the east-wing corridor. He called out to her and she stopped, regarding him in amazement.

"How are you here?" she asked a little breathlessly. "No, you must tell me later, Please, I just wish to leave this house, and at once." She cast her appeal to him in her eyes, and he nodded and led her downstairs and out of the house. He beckoned to the footman holding his horses, and when Tessa had been handed into the carriage, he told the man to have the chaise, which was being walked farther along the drive, sent on to the Stag and Rabbit.

Neither spoke until the gates of Gillane Castle were behind them. Then Jonathan spoke. "That was a damned stupid thing to do, and I suppose it availed you nothing," he said, but not unkindly.

"On the contrary, it served exactly," she responded with spirit. "But I wish it mightn't have been necessary; he is a wretchedly unhappy man and I think most of the blame he placed on you was merely to divert his own judgment of himself. He believes she did take her own life, you know."

"He always did," Jonathan said, his eyes straight ahead on the road. "It was only Connie's dresser that put that notion into his head about murder, but he blamed me enough for her death to convince himself that this could be so, so that I could be punished as properly as he believed I should be. In a way he was right to blame me."

Tessa turned and stared at his profile. "You must never say so," she said with quiet intensity. "I know you are thinking as he does that you made Constance desperate by refusing to forgive her betrayal with Sir Richard, but you could not have done otherwise, and it was Constance who made the choice that she did. If she had had strength of character as well as strength of will, none of what happened would ever have come to pass." And then, remembering that she did not know how it was that he had come to Gillane or known that she would be there, added, "Why are you here, Jon, or better, how? There was no one who knew what I was about except Colin; you *couldn't* have chanced upon him at the inn where I left him."

"No, I found him there because I asked for him. The ostler told me he was there when I stopped for the change and asked after your carriage." He turned slightly toward her as he spoke, and flashed her one of his quick half-smiles.

Tessa found this encouraging, but his words discouraging. "You came after my carriage? But I thought you in Cheltenham?"

"I know, and that is why I came after you," he admitted. "I was told, you see, that you had taken the chance and gone off with McAffe, if not for an elopement, then at least on an illicit assignation away from the prying eyes of the gossips."

"Letty," she said numbly, and then added, "You believed her?" He did not sound angry or upset, which he must have been if he had actually followed her, and she did not know how to read him.

"No," he said, "but you must not be too hard on

your sister; this was more to pay me out than to hurt you. I *did* make a cake of myself, you know, when I found Colin at the inn, but if you are thinking to find him lying bleeding in the back parlour, you won't. Now, let us discuss this no further. We'll work out our motives and be as cross with each other as we like when we get back to the Stag and Rabbit. If we are to understand each other, I would as lief do so when my attention is not being constantly distracted by this abominable road."

As if to emphasize his words, one of the phaeton's wheels went into a rut and tossed Tessa against the side of the carriage. The simple practicality had a soothing effect on Tessa. No one in the throes of jealousy or aggrieved pride would behave in such an unfeelingly pragmatic way, so there was reason to hope that they would be able to talk sensibly and perhaps she would at last be able to say to him the words she had been longing to speak since the night before he had gone away.

The day was too fine for a fire, but Colin was standing before the hearth staring down into it as broodingly as if he watched the flames. He looked up at the sounds of their entrance and at once attacked his cousin. "Dash it, Tess, this was outside of enough. I've always said there was nothing I wouldn't do for you, but this time you've pushed it too far. The next time you get some corkbrained idea in your head, you can dashed well get your own husband to help you carry it off. If you can, which I take leave to doubt, for he's not so easily bullied as I am."

"I don't know about that," Jonathan said meditatively. "She did convince me to marry her against my better judgment, and see where it has brought me." Tessa's eyes flew to his, but she saw laughter there and something else that made her heart beat a bit faster. "You certainly have the right to rip up at Tess," he told Colin, "but I think you might do so a bit more eloquently if you gave what you would say to her more deliberation. The art of the proper set-down is always the better for close application."

"What the devil do you think I've been doing for the last hour and a half?" Colin demanded indignantly. "And I don't care if you don't like it, Hartfield. She was my cousin long before she was your wife."

"Oh, I think she quite deserves it," Jonathan agreed amiably. "The thing is, dear cousin—if I may so address you—I wish you to do it at some other time. I wish to speak with Tess, and you are decidedly *de trop*."

Colin blinked at him for a moment and then flushed slightly. "Yes, of course. I didn't think. I'll wait in the common room, shall I?"

"Why don't you take my phaeton and return to town?" Jonathan suggested. "I'll return with Tess in the chaise."

Colin, who had had quite enough of the Stag and Rabbit, was nothing loath to fall in with this plan. It even put him back in charity with Tessa. He kissed her lightly on the cheek with a watchful eye on her husband, and with a nod and thanks to Jonathan, left them alone in the parlour.

They stood at opposite ends of the room, Tessa near the windows that overlooked the courtyard, and Jonathan still near to the door. He regarded her profile, not nearly as classic as Letitia's or even Constance's had been, and thought her more lovely than any woman he had ever beheld. He wanted more than anything to take her in his arms and kiss away all the troubles that had come between them, but he knew it was not that simple.

Tessa found the silence between them awkward. "I take it you believed Letty that I had gone off illicitly with Colin?" she said, because it was the thing that was in her mind and she felt she had to begin to say something.

"You believed that I wished to make love to Letty," he countered quietly.

"Why did you marry me, Jonathan?" she asked abruptly.

"Why did you marry me?"

"We shall be here all night if you are going to answer my questions with questions," she said tartly.

"You are not answering mine, either," he pointed out. He crossed the room to stand beside her. "You couldn't have married me for my good name, for that was in tatters. My title? An empty thing without your fortune behind it, but you might have had a title in your first season if that was what you wished for. Look at Letty's example. Because you are having my child? That, of course, is the best answer, but the true question this time is why you made love with me in the first place."

"I wished to," she said softly.

"Why?"

"Because I was tired of being on the shelf and thought to throw my lot with the demimonde," she said, deliberately flip. His closeness was disconcerting. She felt a sudden restlessness that she knew was a longing to feel his arms about her and his body again close to hers. Not sure of herself or her reactions to this intimacy, she moved a little away from him, but he too moved. Her back was to the window and she could not again retreat without making the thing very deliberate.

"I married you, Tess," he said levelly, "because I had dishonored you and it was the only thing I could do to give honor back to us both."

"That is honest," she said coolly. This was the plain speaking she had been hoping for, but once again, hardly the words she wished to hear.

"Yes, it is. And I hope you will also believe that I never had designs on your fortune or considered it in making you my wife." This was Dutch comfort to

Tess, but she said nothing and he went on. "I married you because I was three-quarters in love with you and lacked the final quarter only because I would not allow myself to be completely in love with you. It hurt too much to contemplate loving yet another woman who could not love me back."

Tessa could not have been more taken aback. To discover that he loved her, believed that she did not love him as well, and had once been in love with Constance—all in the space of a few moments—was difficult for her to assimilate properly. She focused on the one thing that least touched her. "You loved Constance?"

He smiled rather sadly. "For a time. I haven't the constancy for wearing the willow, I suppose. It didn't last. The world would not credit it—nor, perhaps, would even you—but I think of myself as more of a misfortune hunter than a fortune hunter. It is my lot in life, I think, to fall head over heels in love with beautiful heiresses."

She knew that he was quizzing her a little to ease what must for him be real pain at his admissions. "Why do you suppose that your regard is not returned?" she asked as levelly as she could manage. She placed a diffident hand on his arm, needing the communion of touch for encouragement.

"Is it?" he asked with mild sarcastic surprise. "Unlike Connie, you have never even thrown me the sop of *pretending* love. I don't really mind that, you know. I would rather the truth than a lie. And I know that you are not indifferent to me entirely, for our attraction to each other is unquestionably mutual." He, too, felt the warmth of that simple contact.

"No, I am not indifferent to you, Jon," she said very softly. "From the very beginning, I wanted you, but I didn't know what to do. Like you, I was fearful of the hurt; it was so obvious that you did not wish to marry me, and only did so because I insisted."

"Can't you say it Tess?" he said gently, lightly, almost shyly embracing her. "Then I shall say it for us both: I love you."

The tears that she had not been able to shed in her pain suddenly started to her eyes and spilled onto her cheeks. Partly from happiness and partly from regret at the joy they had wasted over the last two months, they welled from deep inside her. But Jonathan, not privy to the inner workings of her mind, did not understand. He dropped his eyes from hers. "Perhaps I should have kept my tongue, but I can't let happen to us what happened in my first marriage. I rolled myself up in my hurt and never made a push to change our marriage. I consoled myself by saying that Connie hadn't the capacity for love, but I think she loved Cassidy. It might have been me if I'd had more courage, been more determined. I am this time, Tess." He looked up at her again. "Make up your mind to it. You are going to love me, Lady Hartfield, and never regret our odd marriage."

"I could not," Tessa said through her tears, and seeing the tentative smile fade from his eyes, laughed at her own poor choice of words. "I meant I could not regret it. I do love you, Jon—sometimes I think I began to do so the very night of Letty's betrothal ball." She started to tell him of how she had realized as he had that they could not go on in this way and had been so disappointed to find him gone to Cheltenham, but she did not get very far in her explanation. She was swept up tight against him and kissed lovingly, lingeringly, with all the intensity of pent-up passion.

It was an embrace that seemed to her both endless and far too short. When his lips at last left hers, it was only to taste her throat and breast before his mouth again found her own eager lips again.

They remained awhile longer in the parlour, exchanging lovers' words and lovers' caresses, and finally decided to return to town while they had the light to do so, so that they might be this night in their own home. Each could hardly bear the wait to at last start making what had begun with the most unconventional of weddings into the most conventionally happy of marriages.

Afterword

Everyone in the Bellamy and Caster families, including the dowager marchioness, who seldom noticed things that did not pertain to herself, commented on the becoming change they observed in both Lord and Lady Hartfield. Within a sennight of their return from Gillane, it was a common topic of discussion at both dinner tables. Jonathan and Tessa, it was observed, seemed to be so happy and content in their lives that one might have thought that the thing had been a love match after all.

Letitia's wedding at last came about with all the fanfare and attention she could have wished for, and Tessa, who could not blame Letitia for her perfidy, since the result of it had been so splendid, was mindful of her sister's happiness and kept as much to the background as she possibly could.

And after all, Letitia was more than welcome to her limelight as far as Tessa was concerned; she needed no such thing for her own happiness. The only admiration she sought came from one source, and there the supply seemed endless.

Town had not only become increasingly thin of good company by this time, but the days were becoming uncomfortably warm. Tess, town bred as she was, did not mind, but she saw that Jonathan was beginning to chafe to be away from the city and she began to make arrangements for their remove to Boxwood. This was no hardship, however, for she was beginning to feel the effects of her pregnancy—which, as it became increasingly difficult to hide, she had at last confided to her family—and supposed that the country would be more comfortable for the heavy days ahead of her and her eventual lying-in.

The days immediately following Letitia's wedding were completely filled for the entire household at Upper Mount Street with packing and the preparation of closing up the house.

Finally the day arrived for them to leave. Jonathan had spent the first hour after breakfast at the mews seeing to the final details of having their cattle and carriages transported to Boxwood, and he returned to the house to find his wife engaged in a final inventory of their baggage.

"Is all this ours?" he asked incredulously. "I don't recall this much when we came here."

"Because we did not come all at once as we are leaving," Tessa said placidly, not even the harassments of the move sufficient to mar her constant good temper. "But you needn't fear that we are to take every bit of this with us to Boxwood. Only that smaller pile over there is to be loaded into the fourgon. The rest is being taken to Papa's to await our return to find our own house. I think you may order the carriages now if you wish," she concluded with a loving smile.

Quick to oblige, Jonathan summoned a hovering footman and gave the order. They then went upstairs in tandem to retrieve the last of their personal belongings from their bedchambers. The knocker, which had not yet been removed, sounded, checking them both.

Jonathan cursed under his breath. "Who the devil

would call today? All our friends know we are leaving."

"Someone who is not our friend, perhaps," Tessa said with a quizzing smile. "But it needn't concern us." She turned and gave the butler the message to deny them to any callers.

But they had only reached their mutual sitting room when that man tentatively entered and bowed to his master. "I beg your pardon, my lord," he said. "There is a gentleman to see you who claims his business with you is most urgent." He proffered the small tray holding a single card.

Jonathan took it and read it and instantly stiffened. Tessa, who had been observing him, came up beside him. "What is it?"

"This man is from Gillane's firm of solicitors."

Tessa felt herself tense as well. Now that all was so well for them, it was insupportable to think that the Duke of Gillane might yet again intrude in an unhappy way on their lives.

"You'd better see him, Jon," she said quietly. "If there is any difficulty, it would be better to know of it. I still have several things to put into my dressing case, and that will take me a bit of time," she added in case he should wish to use their departure as an excuse to continue to deny himself. But he was of a similar mind and merely nodded and followed the butler out of the room.

The dressing case was finally packed and the footman who informed her that the carriages were ready at the front door had long since gone. The noises that floated up to her from the ground floor told her that even the fourgon was being loaded. Tessa went downstairs again and had the message taken to Jonathan that they were prepared to leave. She waited another quarter-hour in one of the saloons and then decided that she could bear it no longer. In her condition, she told herself, she must not be allowed to suffer such anxiety, and she went directly to the room where Jonathan had received the solicitor, and after only a brief knock, entered it without invitation.

Both men stood as she came into the room. Her anxious glance at her husband told her little more than that he was not put out by her interruption. He introduced her to the short, clerkish man who was called Mr. Cousins. Without further preamble he said baldly, "Gillane died yesterday."

A finger of horror touched Tessa's spine as she remembered the despondent man she had left behind that day in the map room of Gillane Castle. "How?" she asked quickly.

The solicitor cleared his throat. "Apoplexy," he said succinctly. "One of his gardeners disobeyed an order he had given and he fell into a pelter out of which, alas, he never came."

"I am sorry," Tessa said gravely. "I could not like the duke, but I think he was deserving of sympathy."

She looked to her husband to see what he made of this startling but, in its way, not surprising news, but his eyes were particularly metallic today and devoid of discernible expression. "Mr. Cousins had more purpose in coming here today than to bring us that news," he said evenly. "Sit down, Tess, and let him tell you the rest of it."

Mr. Cousins had papers before him and he made a display of gathering them together before speaking. "Simply stated, my lady, it is this: when his grace passed on yesterday, his butler sent a man posthaste to our office to inform us of the unfortunate event because he knew—having been a witness—that our firm held the duke's will, which would, of course, determine the fates of the entire household as soon as the funeral services had been conducted.

"The duke," he continued, "had drawn up a new will not two months ago, with a letter attachment that was to be opened immediately on his death. Briefly the letter summarized the contents of the will and expressed the wish that the heir to the estate be notified of his pending inheritance at once. Lord Hartfield is that heir, my lady."

No unusual event that had occurred to her since the fateful night of Letitia's ball had prepared her for a conclusion to the trouble that would take such a form. She was completely stunned, and her eyes once again flew to her husband's face to gauge his reaction. Jonathan met her eyes and then said firmly, "I don't want it, and I have told Mr. Cousins that I will not accept it. I don't need his damned remorse money."

"I think it was more his way of making it up to you than to ease his own guilt, Jon," Tess said after a moment's reflection. "He could not back away from his accusations against you in life because he could not face the truth, but I really believe he blamed himself far more than you for what happened." She turned again to the solicitor. "Are there other heirs? Will the dukedom go into abeyance?"

"There is an Irish cousin who seldom comes to England and is a wealthy man in his own right," the lawyer replied. "The title will pass to him and also about a third of the estate which is entailed on the title. There are also the usual bequeaths to charities and retainers, but the remainder, I assure you, my lady, is most substantial and goes unconditionally to the Marquis of Hartfield."

Tessa understood Jonathan's feelings, but while thinking them noble, also thought them foolish. "I can see why you would not wish for his fortune, Jon, but you must take it. What you do with it from there is entirely your concern. But," she added with an appraising look cast at him from beneath her lashes, "I think we must look to the future and not hastily allow our emotions to rule our sense."

She thought she saw surprise and a little contempt in his eyes when they met hers. "You mean *I* must not act foolishly," he said tartly. "That damned money never brought anyone who had it anything but grief. We have enough not to be greedy. Why should we want it?"

"It is the people possessing the fortune who bring the grief," she said with quiet reason. "Money is nothing at all in itself but a means to ends."

He met her eyes for a long moment and then returned his attention to the solicitor. "If I must take it, there is nothing more to be said. The details can be worked out at leisure." He rose and held out his hand in dismissal. "You know the direction of Mr. Ryder. The matter may be dealt with through him from here."

Mr. Cousins nodded, bowed his agreement, and left the couple alone.

"You wish me to take that money," Jonathan said, and it was more statement than question. "Why?"

"Because I think it is foolish to whistle down the wind a fortune for the sake of pride," she said flatly. "I see that you think ill of me for my opinion, but I don't apologize for it. My family has not the contempt of the material the way that so many old families such as yours often do. I should not be here today as your wife if my great-grandfather had not risen on his own hard work and merit to become Bishop of Exeter and if all of his sons had not taken his example of using all of their talents and every resource available to them to get on in the world. I don't really care to have the money for us; I am more than content with what we have, but we will soon have a child, and I hope many more. Have we the right to deprive them of what could be the means of advancement to their dreams?"

"Do you realize that people will say that I finally did profit from Constance's death?" he asked musingly. "Don't you think that it might be a constant reminder to us of the duke and all that we have put behind us?"

Tessa shook her head and stood up, holding out her hand to him. "We are keeping the horses waiting," she began, as if she meant to end the conversation, but then suddenly added, "I have another reason for wishing you to take it. I know you did not marry me for my fortune, but I think at times you find it too comfortable and then you dislike it because it does make you feel like a fortune hunter."

He rose too, and took her hand. "At times," he admitted.

"You could repurchase everything that you lost to your father's debt without needing a penny that I have brought you."

"Relieving you of that reluctant burden," he said caustically, but when she looked up at him, she saw that his ready laughter had come into his eyes. "I begin to fear that it is I who have married an adventuress who coyly disguised herself as an heiress to lull my suspicions."

"I am discovered," she cried in a way that would have done credit to Letitia or even the dowager Lady Hartfield, and then threw herself into his arms in a manner that was entirely original to herself.

Having eventually gotten on with the journey, they finally found themselves, as planned, in the chaise on their way to Boxwood. Because it was still on her mind, Tessa renewed their discussion on Jonathan's unexpected inheritance. "Will you mind being so odiously rich?" she asked quizzingly but with an undercurrent of anxiety, for fear that her insistence on his acceptance of it might cause problems for them in the future.

"No," he said, and looking at her, he saw her anxiety and understood it. "No," he said again, more gently. "Shall you mind no longer holding the purse strings?"

She shook her head with a small smile and could not resist saying, "I am not Constance."

He bent his head to kiss her lightly. "I know you are not," he responded, and smiled, knowing that this at last was the end of their doubts for each other and the beginning of their future.

About the Author

Originally from Pennsylvania, Elizabeth Hewitt lives in New Jersey with her husband and cat. She enjoys reading and history, and is a fervent Anglophile. Music is also an important part of her life; she studies voice and sings with her church choir and with the New Jersey Choral Society. THE FORTUNE HUNTER was written to a background of baroque music, as were her two previous novels for Signet's Regency line, BROKEN VOWS and A SPORTING PROPOSITION.